Clan of the Shape-Changers

Clan of the Shape-Changers

Robert Levy

Houghton Mifflin Company
Boston 1994

Library of Congress Cataloging-in-Publication Data

Levy, Robert, 1945–
   Clan of the shape-changers / by Robert Levy.
      p.   cm.
   Summary: Having inherited the power to change into any kind of
animal, sixteen-year-old Susan joins the fight against the greedy
shaman Ometerer, who is attempting to steal this secret from her
people and then destroy them.
   ISBN 0-395-66612-0
   [1. Fantasy.]   I. Title.
PZ7.L5836C1   1994   92-36010
[Fic] — dc20   CIP
                    AC

Printed in the United States of America

VB   10 9 8 7 6 5 4 3 2 1

In memory of Belle Mintz

and

To my editor, Audrey Bryant,
who read something that was and saw
something that could be.
For all your help, thank you.

Clan of the
Shape-Changers

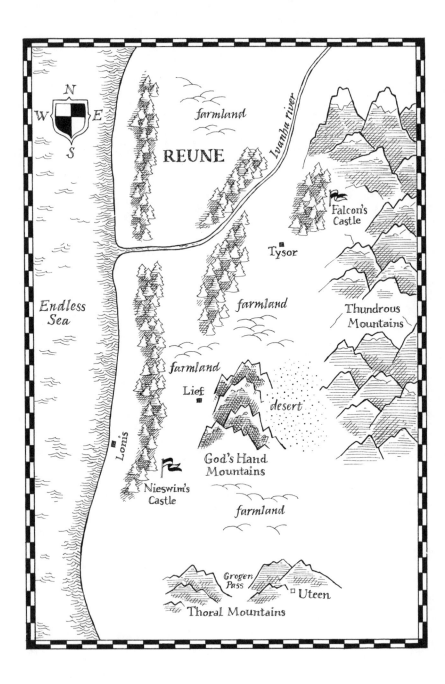

Chapter 1

"Run, Susan," whispered Susan's father as he died. And the terrified girl ran.

"Get that child!" shouted one of the soldiers.

Run, thought Susan. *Run!* Her legs raced — up-down, up-down — she breathed harder as she jumped over a stream and darted into the forest. But she was only eight and couldn't outdistance a grown man. She looked back and saw the soldier only a few steps behind.

"No! Leave me alone!" Susan faced the woods and willed her feet to move faster. But they couldn't. The gap narrowed. Out of the corner of her eye, Susan saw him leap. *No!* her mind screamed as the large body hurtled toward her.

"Oof!" Instantly, Susan's eyes popped open. Instead of the soldier, all she saw was a mass of brown fur pushing against her face. "Get off me." However, her arms were pinned between her and the fur. She couldn't move and Farrun, her wolf, knew it. As soon as he heard her voice, he inched down until his head was even with hers. Then he began licking her face.

"All right," said Susan, turning her head sideways to

keep his tongue away from her mouth. "I'm up. I'm up. I'm not dreaming anymore."

But Farrun didn't listen. He rarely listened when it came to things like this, and, being well over a hundred pounds, he didn't have to. He finished licking and stretched his front paws straight out, tucking his nose between Susan's head and the wall.

"Will you get off me!" Susan finally managed to get her arms free. When he didn't move, she scratched him behind the ears. Since yelling didn't move him, she tried a different tack — pleading. "Please. You're not a cub now; it's getting hard to breathe."

Farrun lifted his head and yawned. Then he licked her ear, put his head down, and pushed against her hand. He liked being scratched.

Susan was about to roll over when a trumpet sounded. Farrun quickly struggled to get up. His paws pressed into her stomach — Susan's breath flew out. "Will you be careful! How many times do I have to tell you you don't weigh ten pounds anymore!"

Farrun sort of growled as he jumped to the floor. He had another job to do now, protecting her, and the quicker he was on his feet, the better. He knew what that trumpet meant just as well as Susan did. A king's messenger was coming into Uteen.

"I'll bet we're in for trouble," said Susan, putting on a woolen dress. "Whenever a king's messenger comes into the Thoral Mountains, it always means trouble."

Combing her shoulder-length brown hair with her fingers, she walked into the morning light. Most of the villagers were already in the center of the town, crowding around four men on horseback. Susan saw her father, Maklin, and forced her way through the crowd until she stood next to him at the front of the circle. Being sixteen helped her get away with pushing; most adults tended to excuse the impolite behavior of a "child." Having a full-grown wolf next to her didn't hurt either.

"That's not a messenger," she said to her father, "that's a shaman! I wonder why he's here?"

"Shh, girl," answered Maklin. "We'll hear in a minute. Don't be so impatient."

Susan didn't have to wait. The white-robed shaman with a shaved head, the sign that he was no longer a novice but a full shaman, took a scroll from a leather case. Holding both hands in front of his face and sliding the bottom part of the scroll down, he straightened his back and sat tall in the saddle. Never once did he look at the people standing around him. He did, however, glance at one of the soldiers who stood behind him.

"Stand back!" said one man, inching his horse toward the villagers. "Stand back!"

Not waiting for the villagers to move, the shaman began reading. "Let it be known that A'aster, King of Reune, voice of the gods in our land . . ."

"We've heard that before," said Maklin. "Get on with it!"

The shaman looked again at one of the soldiers and the man's horse stepped toward Maklin. Farrun shoved his way past Susan, growled, and raised his hackles. Exposed rows of sparkling white teeth made the horse stop. The shaman began again.

"Let it be known that A'aster, King of Reune, voice of

the gods in our land, and supreme defender of justice, hereby decrees the following:

"After long discourse with Ometerer, Defender of the True Magic, leader of the shamans, King A'aster has decided that magic of a vile and evil nature is the cause of the severe droughts that plague Reune. Ometerer has concluded that the source of the magic comes from witches living within the borders of Reune, witches whose ancestors once tried and failed to seize the throne."

Susan heard the villagers behind her begin to whisper, and when the shaman continued he had to raise his voice. As he read the first few words, the soldiers drew their swords and laid them across their saddles.

"These witches, all bearing the same mark of their ancestors, are now being caught and questioned by shamans who have received their instructions from Ometerer himself." The shaman had to stop because many of the people, Maklin included, began shouting.

"Silence!" yelled the shaman. "Those who are not witches have nothing to fear." The shouts became mumbles; the mumbles became silence. Susan backed away to hide behind her adopted father. She knew about the mark. The shaman lowered his scroll and, for the first time, looked at the people.

"King A'aster, acting as defender of justice, and with the complete agreement of Ometerer, realizes that not everyone with the witches' mark is a witch. Therefore" — once again he lifted the scroll — "all people bearing that mark are ordered to return to the village of their birth, be that within the Thoral Mountains or not. They shall be branded on their foreheads as a sign proclaiming they have

4

been questioned and found innocent." A low din began to rise. The shaman lowered the scroll. "It is further ordered that all those bearing the witches' mark are forbidden to marry or bear children. It is the divine will of King A'aster that within one generation the mark of the witch clan will forever be wiped from the face of his kingdom."

The people charged. Susan saw the three soldiers yanked off their horses before they could raise their swords. The shaman screamed, "in note . . ." but he never finished because dozens of hands hauled him off his horse. Susan turned, covering her ears and pushing against the crowd. "Come on, Farrun!" She ran toward a path that led into the mountains.

Farrun knew where to go and took the lead. When he stopped, the girl caught up and sat next to him. She hugged him tightly.

For the longest time, Susan was silent, stroking Farrun's head and staring out from their seat, a cliff edge overlooking the village. "What am I going to do? I have to leave in three weeks to prove myself. How am I going to do that now?" Farrun didn't answer, but he did move his head so Susan would scratch another spot. "I can't go. I just can't. What will Father say?"

"What will Father say about what?" said a voice behind her. Farrun never moved. Long before Maklin appeared, the wolf had recognized his scent and knew Susan was in no danger.

"What happened . . . to them?" she asked when he sat next to her.

Maklin plucked a single blade of grass and began chewing on it. But he didn't answer.

"Why did the people have to . . . Couldn't they have . . ."

But the only answer he gave was to shake his head slowly. When he finally did speak, he repeated what he had said before. "What will I say about what?"

"Oh, Father, you know. I have to . . . my testing period. I'm supposed to leave in three weeks. How can I go now?"

"The same way you would have gone if the shaman had never come to Uteen. You're going to walk."

"Stop teasing!" Maklin pulled his daughter close and kissed her head. "Please tell me what happened to them?"

Maklin still didn't answer. "You know, Susan, you have a rare gift. Do you think the Elders would have left the power behind when they vanished if they didn't want it used? For almost four hundred years, since the time of the rebellion, those with the power have left the Thorals and done what they could to help people. You heard what the shaman said. Ever since Ometerer became head shaman, A'aster's rule has become more and more oppressive. I'm surprised A'aster hasn't declared himself a god and ordered the people to build temples for him. Child, in the past several years, he's become the worst king we've had in ages. If there ever was a time when you were needed, this is it. I just wish I had the power, too. Then I'd go with you."

"I do, too," she answered. "Then you would have taught me instead of Rillan."

"And what's wrong with Rillan?"

"Nothing, really. It's just that sometimes he says the same things over and over again."

"Such as?"

"'Never use your power in front of anyone who isn't clan or family.'"

"What's wrong with that?"

"Nothing, except it's so obvious. If he told me once, he told me a hundred times. No one would ever do that!"

"Susan, I'm not clan, but my sister is. No one knows where the Elders came from, but their power has been in Reune for almost a thousand years. What may be obvious to you wasn't always obvious. That's why Rillan repeats himself so much. You'll thank him for that when you return after being on your own for a while.

"But I'm not ready. It's been only four years since Rillan discovered I had the power. He hasn't had an apprentice in over ten years, and he once told me it takes at least five to train someone fully."

"Rillan thinks you're ready for the testing period, and I trust his judgment. Come on or you'll be late for your lesson. I don't want him to think I've raised a lazy daughter." Reluctantly, she got up.

Susan was very busy for the next three weeks. Rillan went over years of learning, asking questions, listening to answers, and making her practice. On the morning of her final day, Susan stood before him.

"You've learned everything you have to know, and you've learned it well. You are prepared," said Rillan. "Even with the new law, you are prepared."

"But . . ." started Susan.

"No buts," he interrupted.

"All right," whispered Susan.

"Just remember what you've learned. Think before you act. Never use your power lightly."

"Yes, Rillan."

"And above all, once you leave the Thorals, never . . ."

"Use my power without thinking first or in front of anyone," Susan finished.

Rillan looked at her through squinted eyes. Then he showed a broad smile and hugged her tightly.

Early that evening, before the sun dipped beneath the farthest peak and the twin moons poked their heads into the sky, Maklin, Susan, and Farrun stood on the cliff edge looking over their village. Long, dark shadows covered the valley, making the houses below invisible. Susan had said her goodbyes to everyone else and wanted to say it to Maklin here, her favorite place.

He held her cheeks between his hands as he spoke. "It seems like only yesterday I first saw you, a skinny bundle of rags that no one wanted, shivering in the road. I've had four years since you started your schooling to get used to your leaving, and though the power *is* needed, I don't like feeling I'm sending you away."

"You're not sending me away, Father. You've told me often enough that it's no use having the power if we don't use it for the good of everyone. I have to stay away, living by my own decisions, doing what I can to help those without the power. If one of the clan had been near my house when the tax collectors came, maybe my birth parents wouldn't have been killed. It's my time to go. It's just that with only four years of training, and this new law, I'm not very sure of myself. I think I'm afraid."

"Never be ashamed of being afraid, Susan, as long as you have a reason to be. And you have one now. Be very careful, Daughter. You know I couldn't love you more if you were my own blood, and I don't want anything to happen to you."

Susan opened her arms and held him.

"It's time. It will take you over a week to leave the Thorals. Be careful and come home as soon as you can. I'll miss you."

Susan kissed him, picked up her travel-pack, and started walking.

"Take good care of her, Farrun."

Susan turned and waved only once, knowing if she did it again, she might not go. She didn't have to, but unless she did, she would always hear the word "coward" whispered behind her. "Come on, Farrun. This is my testing period, and when I come home healthy and wiser because I've been on my own, everyone will know I earned the right to use the Elders' power. Missing home will make the time move slower, right?" Farrun didn't answer. He just walked a few feet in front, turning his head to make sure she was behind him and searching for trouble, as he always did.

Susan chose the longer way out of the mountains. She and Farrun wanted to avoid all the villages between Uteen and the farmlands that started at their base. Even though no one who lived in the Thoral Mountains would accuse her of being a witch, there might be other shamans and king's soldiers in some of the villages who would. Sooner or later that would have to happen; there was no way she could hide the Elders' mark. But the longer that day could be put off, the better she liked it. Rillan had assured her she was ready to survive her testing, but Susan wasn't convinced.

"What do you think, Farrun," she said, petting him on

the shoulder as they walked. "Do you think I'm nervous because Maklin said I have to be careful or do you think it's because I'm not so sure of myself?"

Farrun looked up at her. He did that sometimes, and it always made Susan believe he understood every word she said. He jumped up, resting his front paws on her shoulders. While Susan rubbed his back, the big wolf licked her face in long, wet strokes.

"Well," she said, letting him wash the dirt from her, "at least I won't be alone. Father told me that some of my clan brothers and sisters decided to live in Reune after their testing was over. Of course, finding them won't be easy." Susan was taught early in her training that all people who possess the power have the mark. But few people who have the mark have the power.

Farrun pinched her earlobe between his teeth and growled. Then he licked it once and sat looking at her.

"You're right," she said. "What do I need other clan members for? I have you, don't I?"

Farrun nudged his head into her stomach, pushing her farther down the path.

"You're right again. We've got to get going."

The weather stayed warm, the paths Farrun chose were never too steep, and game was always abundant. Farrun had no trouble catching their meals. The beginning of her testing period turned out to be nothing more than a pleasant outing with her best friend.

Once they left the Thoral Mountains, the land gradually flattened out. As they headed northwest, the hills were replaced with long stretches of plains covered in tall grass that waved in the wind. Farrun led the way, skirting the villages whose people farmed that land. Susan didn't want to meet anyone until she reached her first goal, the Endless Sea that touched Reune's entire western border. So they hid whenever they had to. Hiding was easy because where the land was not plowed and planted, the high grass hid anyone who did not want to be seen.

At the end of the third week, the land began to rise. Hills covered with trees and tall green bushes rose up out of the ground, making a natural boundary for the end of the grasslands. Farrun ran ahead of Susan, racing in and out of the trees. They were nothing compared to those in the Thorals, but in his own way, Farrun was telling Susan he missed their home. Several times he playfully jumped on her, pushing her to the ground — he wanted her to use her power. He wanted a playmate, one of his own kind. But whenever he did that, Susan would laugh and blow in his face.

"I don't want to change, Farrun. If we come across anyone, I want them to see us as we are, understand?"

Farrun would lick her nose — his way of saying it was all right — until the next time he jumped on her, she said no, and he licked her nose again.

Two days later, Susan felt a moist breeze against her cheeks. As she ran up the last hill, she heard a soft rhythmic pounding. She reached the top and saw it. More water than she ever imagined spread out before her. It was in constant motion, making small hills and valleys far from the shore. The waves, continuous rolls of white foam, made a mesmerizing roar as they rushed toward the beach.

She sat on her high hill staring at the blue-green water, hardly aware that Farrun had poked his head between her folded arms. She automatically began petting him.

"Look at it, Farrun. Isn't it . . . isn't it beautiful?"

Farrun's only answer was to lean heavily into the scratch.

Susan remembered the awed feeling she had the first time she saw the Thorals up close many years ago. The water's spell was just as hypnotizing. Susan's shoulders twitched as chills crossed her back. Her face flushed, her eyes opened wide. "I'll remember this sight forever."

An hour later, they rose and walked the sands of the beach, continuing northward. Carrying her shoes, she picked up shells as the water touched the bottoms of her feet before slowly rolling away. Several times, she tried to get Farrun to play "fetch" with pieces of driftwood that littered the beach.

"Go get it, Farrun," she'd say, throwing a stick into the water.

But Farrun only watched the wood as it sailed into the surf. He loved playing games, but if he went into the water, he couldn't get to Susan quickly if he had to.

They left the beach only when hunger forced them back into the hills. Though Susan could hunt for herself, she preferred to let Farrun do it. She didn't want to use her power to kill, even if it was for food. Her job was to prepare the fire and cook what Farrun brought.

On their third day of walking along the beach, Susan saw smoke from a nearby village. "Let's see if they'll let us stay there awhile. I'd like to learn how to sail those boats we've seen."

Farrun stopped.

"Well, in a place as remote as this, maybe the people haven't heard about the king's new proclamation. If they haven't, I'll tell them my parents owed money to our local lord and I ran away to prevent being sold into slavery."

Farrun tilted his head.

"It's the best story I can think of." When he sort of half yawned, half growled, she continued. "All right, if they've heard about the law, I'll say I am obeying it, returning to the village I was born in. Maybe they'll still let me stay awhile."

Farrun turned and started walking toward the houses. When he growled, Susan knew something was wrong.

People on the shore were shouting and pointing toward the water while several men were hastily dragging a boat toward the surf. Her eyes followed the pointed fingers to a small figure bouncing up and down in the water. "Someone's drowning!" Susan looked at the men who were just now beginning to row. "They'll never get there in time."

This isn't good, Susan thought. *I won't have time to think of a story explaining how I got there before the men. Rillan told me never to use my power before thinking about it, before having a plan. But I don't have a choice! The person will die if I don't do something!* She reached down and pulled her dress over her head. Being undyed, natural wool, it would become part of her when she used the power — and reappear on her body when she finished. But explaining how she reached the person first would be hard; explaining a heavy wet dress on her would be impossible.

Farrun tried to block her way.

13

"Stay," she told him, as she kicked off her shoes and dropped her dress on the sand. In one smooth motion, she jumped over Farrun and plunged into the water. Its chill grabbed her. Its salt burned her eyes. But the girl didn't think about that as she rose to the top and swam into the waves. She was a good swimmer, but without using her power she would never reach the person in time. She took a deep breath and dived.

"Using the power is never easy and only with the greatest concentration can you do it in haste." Those were some of the words Rillan had spoken dozens of times. Now, as Susan swallowed seawater and broke the surface coughing, she was glad he had. Before diving again, she took another deep breath, clamped her lips together, and went under the surface.

"Concentrate," Rillan's voice said. "Think of what you wish to become and force your body to mold itself into it. But be careful. Don't let the natural instinct of your new form control you. Always remember who you are and what you want to accomplish."

Susan concentrated, trying to hurry the various steps of changing. First her legs. They sealed, dissolved into each other, and within seconds a long black fin moved up and down behind her waist.

Now my body, thought Susan. Once again, she poked her head out of the water. Speeding rapidly as her tail propelled her, she held her breath again and went back under.

Change my body, she thought. *Change!*

Her arms shrank — vanished into her shoulders — her chest contracted — lungs changed into gills, and Susan was almost done.

14

"Careful," Rillan's voice echoed in her still-human head. "Don't get stuck in transition. It sometimes happens even to experienced clanspeople when they're excited."

Change, Susan thought for the last time. But nothing happened. A grotesque creature, a large black fish with a human head, swam farther away from the shore. Susan closed her eyes. She forgot about the need for speed — she forgot about the floundering person. She thought only about her job.

Her face narrowed; her chest sucked up her neck and her vision cleared. Just before she completely changed into the fish that now silently flew through the water, Susan had one last thought. *I'm doing it. For the first time, when it really counts, I'm using my power. I am a Shape-Changer!*

Chapter 2

SHAL-LOW-WA-TER-GO-DEE-PER, thought the part of Susan's mind that was now a fish.

No! screamed Susan's mind, fighting for control. *There, that's a boy who's drowning. Go to him. Go to him!*

BIG-SPLASH-BOAT-PEO-PLE-COME-GO-GO-DEE-PER-BE-SAFE, thought the Susan-fish.

Arguing with her mind was not new to Susan. Whenever a Shape-Changer used the power to become another form, part of the changer's mind became the animal's mind. That part tried to do whatever the natural instinct of the animal told it to. It spoke to the human part of the changer's mind.

No! thought Susan. *No go deeper. Go to the boy. Listen to me. Go to the boy.*

The Susan-fish veered and headed for the boy. Just before she reached him, Susan broke her concentration. She thought of herself as a full human, and in one smooth motion became wholly herself. Returning to one's original shape was always the easiest part of changing.

By the time she broke the surface, she held the boy in her arms. Susan looked around as the waves bobbed her

and, holding the boy's head above the water, began swimming.

But the boy was heavy. She kicked her legs and paddled with her free arm. Yet for each stroke forward, the waves pulled her back two. She coughed. Water forced its way into her throat and she felt herself sinking. Susan dropped the boy for a second while she used both arms to lift her head above the water. Then she grabbed him again.

Two men dived from the approaching boat and when they were close, Susan released the boy. One man swam for him while the other dove, coming to the surface behind her. His arm wrapped around her chest and he turned her on her back. She tried to pull away, but the grip became tighter. "I've got you, understand?" he said. Susan stopped fighting and the man swam with her. When they reached the boat, hands lifted her up. She coughed and spit out water, but after feeling solid wood against her skin, she relaxed.

Susan was tired. Changing shape so quickly had taken a lot of her strength. Trying to swim with the boy had robbed her of the rest. She coughed again as someone draped a blanket over her.

"You're safe now," she heard just before she closed her eyes and darkness overtook her.

Farrun's growl woke her.

"How can I give her medicine if that wolf won't let me near her? Get it away!

"Maybe she doesn't need your medicine, old man," she heard. "This is my house. She and her wolf are welcome, no matter what you say about a wolf not being a suitable pet. He didn't snap at me when I carried her here or when I laid her in bed and covered her. Maybe the wolf knows better than you. Not everyone in Lonis treats your word as the king's law. One day they may even decide you're more nuisance than anything else and throw you out."

The other man's voice became cracked and shrill, telling Susan its owner was an old man. "The law will punish you, Caster. That I promise you."

"This is my house, Vincent. That girl saved my nephew, and if you even think of getting near her, I won't stop her wolf from tearing you to pieces."

Susan moved her legs and the rustling sound of the coarse blanket silenced Caster. Farrun, who sat next to the bed, did not object when Caster came closer.

"I'm sorry we woke you," he said. "You should have slept longer."

"I'm fine," answered Susan, sitting up. But as soon as she realized she was naked, she lay down again and pulled the blanket up.

Caster smiled and shook his head. "You must have traveled a long way because your dress was torn in many places. My wife is outside mending it. We'll wait there until she's done."

"I must question her now," said Vincent. "I must know how she did it. No one saw her swimming for the boy. Where did she come from? How did she save him?"

"How do you think? With strong arms and legs, that's how. Now, I told her we'll wait outside." Just to make sure Vincent agreed, he pushed the man toward the door.

As soon as everyone had left, Farrun put his front paws on the edge of the bed. He made small yelping noises as he wagged his tail and licked her face.

"I'm fine, Farrun, really I am."

But Farrun didn't take her word. He jumped on the bed, carefully putting his paws near the edge. He stopped licking her and pushed his nose against her neck and then her chest. When he had finished sniffing, he jumped down and sat looking at her.

"See, I told you. What can you tell me about Vincent? I didn't see him at all." She leaned over and rested her head on her bare arm, watching Farrun.

Farrun walked to the door, raised his hackles, and growled. Then he returned.

Susan scratched her head. *The last time Farrun had acted like that was when the shaman came to Uteen. The shaman!* "Farrun, is Vincent a shaman?"

Farrun's tail moved slowly back and forth.

"I used my power near a shaman! Now what are we going to do? What can we tell them?" Farrun didn't answer and there was silence. "I could have stayed a fish and kept the boy above water until the men came. Then no one would have seen me. I guess that's what Rillan meant when he said I should think about the consequences of what I do before I do it."

Farrun tilted his head and then licked her nose.

"But if I had taken the time to think about that before I changed, the boy might have died. How am I supposed to know when to . . ." The rest of her sentence was cut off when the door opened and a woman appeared. The woman remained by the door, afraid of Farrun, afraid to come into the hut.

"He won't hurt you," said Susan, petting the wolf's

19

head, but the woman was not reassured. She tiptoed into the room, draped Susan's dress over the table, and hurried out, closing the door behind her.

As Susan dressed, she took a good look around the empty house. It was a large, single-room hut with grass and mud for walls and upright logs sunk into the earth holding up the roof. There were two windows, neither facing the sea. One looked out into the village, and the other to the distant forested hills. In the center of the room was a table with two stools and a chair. A fireplace was in one corner, and two beds, including the one she had been on, were in another. The beds were nothing more than wooden platforms covered with hay. Small blocks of wood under each edge kept them several inches above the dirt floor. The rest of the house was bare and reminded her of another one, one burned ages ago. But this was not the time for old memories; she had a shaman to worry about.

"Come on, Farrun, let's get this over with. But be on your guard. If we have to run, I'll head for the hills and you take care of the shaman. You think you can?"

Farrun jumped up, wagging his tail and putting his front paws on her shoulders while licking her cheek.

"I wish I believed in me as much as you do. But I'll get better, just you wait."

Farrun dropped to the floor and poked his head into her stomach with more force than he usually used. Then he turned to the door, raised his hackles again, and snapped at the air.

"I wasn't afraid when I saved the boy because I knew what I was doing. I knew nothing would happen to me while I was the fish. This isn't the same because I don't know what's going to happen. I can't afford to make a mistake when I talk to the shaman."

Farrun pushed her again, this time toward the door.

"You're right," she said. "We can't stay in here forever."

Shielding her eyes from the bright sunlight with her hand, Susan watched the villagers gathering around her and recognized Caster. He was a small chubby man with large arms, a wide, thick neck, and thinning dark hair. Vincent, a frail man with a dirty white robe, shaved head, and sparse beard, stood next to him.

"We'd like to thank you for saving Dunjer's life," said one man. "We couldn't have reached him in time."

"I'm glad I could help," Susan answered, lowering her hand.

"Look. Look at her!" screamed Vincent. "She bears the mark of the witch!"

Several of the villagers backed away as Vincent stepped closer. "Kill her before she casts her evil upon us!" he shouted. When no one moved, he turned and faced the people. "What are you waiting for? Can't you see she has the green eyes of the witch clan! She must die! Strike her now, before she has time to run. And the wolf, too, must also die. What runs with a witch, must be part witch!"

"I am not a witch!" said Susan. "It's true I have green eyes, but I'm not a witch. Over half the people in the Thoral Mountains have green eyes."

"Then what are you doing here?" said Vincent, rubbing his hands together. "Tell us that, witch."

Susan stepped back and rested one hand on Farrun's

head. "I have to return to where I was born. That's the new law. They're going to . . . they're going to . . ."

"You don't have to say anything else," said Caster. "We heard the law. I told you, Vincent, it's a stupid law. Now I hope everyone here knows why. You know what's going to happen to her when she gets there, don't you? You know what kind of life she's going to live?"

"I don't believe you," Vincent stormed. "There are no villages near here, and Lonis is certainly not your home." He took two steps toward Susan. Farrun pulled his lips back, exposing sharp, canine teeth and growled a low, soft growl that dared Vincent to step closer. The old man backed up.

"The law didn't say I have to return right away," said Susan. "I wanted to see the ocean. I've always wanted to see the ocean so I'm taking my time."

"You take all the time you want," said Caster.

"No," said Vincent. "The law did not say take your time. The law . . ."

Caster suddenly turned and threw the old man down, placing a foot on his neck. While Vincent coughed and feebly struck at the leg pinning him to the earth, Caster spoke to Susan. "Four years ago, while I was away, pleading our case to Lord Nieswim because we couldn't pay the village taxes, my son was born. This creature called him a witch because he had green eyes, and you," he said to the rest of the people, "allowed him to kill my boy." Vincent tried to answer but only a high squeak came out of his mouth. Caster pressed his foot down harder. "Since then, I've wanted nothing more than to see you dead. If you don't lie still, I'll do it now!" Vincent's hands clutched

Caster's ankles, but he had no strength to shove the foot away. He lay there, breathing loudly as the foot cut off most of the air. The shaman did manage to lift his right shoulder and twist his body. His head turned slightly, and when Caster pressed harder, Vincent's left cheek was plastered in the sand. He breathed in short, quick breaths as one eye glared up at Susan.

"If anyone tries to harm this girl, I'll kill him, understand?" said Caster. All the villagers remained still except for three who stepped toward Caster. Farrun faced the men, and when he snarled, they quickly moved away.

Caster lifted his foot. Vincent sat up, rubbing his neck with both hands and taking long, noisy breaths. "Don't try any of your magic, either," continued Caster. "Not unless you want to say your spells forever because when you stop, I will kill you!"

Magic? What magic can he have? He's only a hateful old man.

"Listen to me," said Vincent as he got up. "Am I not the king's voice in this village? Haven't I been telling you for years, even before A'aster came to his senses and ordered the witch-eyes home, that the witches are causing our problems? Why do you think the rains fall less each year, making our crops harder to grow? Why do you think our nets come up half empty, with just enough to feed ourselves and nothing left to trade for the things we cannot make? It's her and her people. Since the green-eyed army came down from the Thorals and tried to conquer all of Reune four hundred years ago, they have plotted against the rightful rulers of our country. They want our land, and when we're too weak to fight for it, they'll destroy A'aster and Ometerer and take Reune for themselves. Am I not a full shaman? I order you to put her to death!"

"I'm warning you, Vincent," Caster said. "This girl will not be harmed."

"My father said I should never stay where I'm not wanted," interrupted Susan. "If you can spare some food, we'll leave. I still have a long way to go."

"Why aren't you listening to me!" screamed Vincent. "She's not going home! She's going to do more magic — magic that will eventually kill you."

Caster stood next to Susan and Farrun. Slowly, quietly, the crowd began to vanish; some walked toward the beach, others disappeared into their houses. When all but three had gone, Vincent stepped forward, though Farrun's growl still kept him several arm's lengths away. "They won't listen to me, witch, but you will. First, I will tell those of my order you are here. Ometerer himself, Defender of the True Magic, is close by. Then I will hunt you down with men who aren't cowards. The next time we meet, I will burn you and bury your ashes deep in the ground. After your death, my order will rid our country of all of your kind!" Vincent clenched his teeth and pulled back his lips like an angry animal. He raised an arm that had barely enough flesh to cover the bone and pointed a crooked finger at the girl. "Leave if you will, witch. Only remember there's no place to hide." Susan could almost touch the hate coming from this man, and that made the hair on her arms bristle. Without thinking, she stepped back. "Beware, girl. I will come for you!"

Though he was an old man, Vincent stomped off with the speed of someone Susan's age. The three men who had waited for him had to run to catch up. Susan let out a deep breath; she was very relieved when they finally disappeared.

Caster fed her and begged her to stay, but Susan refused. "Vincent and the men who left with him will return. I don't want to cause you any more trouble."

"Those three," muttered Caster. "They're the worst fishermen in the village. Just like them to blame others because their nets come up empty," he said as he packed some bread into Susan's travel-pack. "If they spent more time learning how to cast their nets properly and less time listening to Vincent, they wouldn't be so eager to believe the shamans' garbage. I'm sorry for this. I don't understand how anyone in his right mind can still blame green-eyed people for a war that ended ages ago. Even newborn babies are . . ." He stopped, took a breath, and waited a minute before continuing. "Isn't there anything I can do to repay you for saving my nephew's life? This bread certainly isn't enough."

"You stood up for me. That was enough."

"It will have to be if you insist on leaving, but if you ever change your mind, law or no law, you have a friend in this house."

Susan waved goodbye as she walked through the center of the village, making sure everyone could see her and Farrun leave. They headed north and east out of Lonis; Vincent and the men with him had walked southeast toward the tree-covered hills. Susan didn't want to run into them. Several hours later, hidden in ever-darkening shadows as the sun began reaching for the low horizon, the travelers stopped. She sat on the ground and petted Farrun's head as it rested in her lap. "What are we going to do? If I spend my testing time hiding from everyone, I won't learn anything, will I? My ancestors wouldn't be very proud of me if they knew I didn't use their power just because things were getting difficult."

Farrun looked at her with half-closed eyes and yawned. Suddenly, he looked at Susan and growled.

"Don't you growl at me," she said, lightly tapping his nose. But Farrun didn't listen. He poked his snout close to her cheek and snapped the air next to Susan's face. Then he growled, licked her cheek a few times, and put his head in her lap waiting for more scratches.

"I don't understand you. Oh, Farrun, why can't you talk to me? Why isn't there a magic that can let us really talk to each other?"

Farrun leaned into the hand Susan was scratching with. Then he growled again, or sort of growled.

"Are you thinking about Vincent?" she asked.

All he did was move his head higher into her lap.

"Vincent . . . Vincent . . ." said Susan. "What did he say? He was going to tell Ometerer. Ometerer! He's the leader of all the shamans. If we knew what their plans were . . ." Now Farrun did look up.

"Thank you," said Susan, rubbing both sides of his head briskly. "But can we catch up with him and follow without being seen?"

Farrun sat and poked his head into her chest, knocking her over.

"All right. Just remember, no playing. We have work to do."

Susan tied her travel-pack on Farrun's back, and when it was secure, stepped away.

Rillan had explained that using the power was never easy, except in one instance. "For some unknown reason," he told her, "each Shape-Changer has one special shape, one special animal. Once you master the power, you can change into your animal quickly and easily. When you do that, you don't suffer a loss of energy." Susan's shape, much to Farrun's delight, was a she-wolf.

She hardly felt the change the power forced her body to make because she had become this shape many times during her lessons. But each time, the thrill was just the same. This was her form, she owned it, and when she was her Susan-wolf, she felt as if she were grown up. As her arms grew thick and her legs shortened, Susan felt her power. Her face narrowed and lengthened, her chest became small and compact, her muscles bulged, pressing against her sprouting fur. In half the time it took her to become the Susan-fish, the change was complete. Farrun waited until the change was finished before prancing around her. He licked her face and smelled her. He put his paws on her and forced her to sit. He rubbed his cheek against hers and licked some more.

Susan snapped at him. When she was her wolf, she never had to fight the instincts of a real wolf. She was wholly Susan and wholly the wolf at the same time, and the Susan-wolf knew they had to go.

Farrun understood and started out. The Susan-wolf followed the brisk pace he set. She loved being a wolf. As if a balloon had popped inside her head, her senses were suddenly alive. She tasted the air and could tell what animals walked upwind of her. Her ears picked out the slightest sounds, and the trees and bushes, lit only in the dim light of the twin moons that had just appeared over the horizon, became daylight-clear to her new oval eyes as she raced effortlessly south. Behind the trees to their right, smoke from the village fires speared the night sky, but the sea wind wouldn't allow it to reach the clouds. It blew the fish-scented smoke into spiny fingers that reached for the now black woods. The distance it had taken Susan hours to walk was covered in a few racing minutes.

When Susan was in her human form, Farrun listened to her most of the time. But in her wolf shape, it was usually the other way around. Farrun stopped and Susan stayed behind as his head moved from side to side, breathing the air, tasting the smells it carried. When he found what he wanted, he turned and picked up speed. Within minutes, they saw the glow of a fire; they had found their prey. She and Farrun stalked the camp like overgrown cats looking for mice, their ears back, their stomachs almost touching the ground. Farrun stopped behind a low bush, but Susan crawled around it and kept going. Though she could make out what Vincent and the others were saying, she wanted to get closer. *I'm a Shape-Changer. How can Vincent hurt me when he doesn't know I'm here?* Farrun came from behind and pushed his head into her shoulders. But instead of retreating as he wanted, the Susan-wolf stayed where she was, settling down with her head on her front paws, well out of the circle of firelight. Farrun, who knew better than to make any noise, reluctantly stayed next to her.

"What did I tell you?" she heard Vincent say as he threw the last of his supper into the fire. "The witches are coming out of the Thoral Mountains. I thank the gods I'm alive for the beginning of their extermination. Soon, the witches and all their kin will be dead."

"But only those who weren't born there are leaving," said one of the men.

"You are a fool, Steven," answered Vincent. "Right now, Ometerer has ordered every witch questioned. But it's only a matter of time before he discovers that questioning them will do no good. Witches are witches and all the talk in Enstor won't change that. There is nothing the witches know that is worth knowing. Soon, even Ometerer, Defender of the True Magic, will come to realize that. Then he will order them killed, not brought to him alive. As a matter of fact, if the Thorals weren't so hard to get into with our horses, and so easy to defend, the witch clan would have been destroyed a long time ago. When Ometerer is ready, he will march on Grogen Pass. Then we will take the Thorals."

"But must she die so soon?" asked another man. "She's a pretty one. I'd like to get to know her before she burns."

Vincent jumped up. "You're no brighter than Steven, Kenar," he said, spitting into the fire and waving his arms madly. The fire was at his back and all Susan could see was a black shadow standing behind the jumping flame. A cold chill raced through her, and she felt the fur along her neck stand up. Vincent would kill her the next time he saw her. And Kenar, he would . . . She began to inch backward, rustling some leaves under her hind legs. Farrun leaned

29

close and licked her ear. He didn't want her to move. Susan calmed.

"Don't you listen, Kenar? How many times have I told you that you cannot play with witches, even the young, pretty ones? Why do you think Caster and his wife are on our list? Why do you think his brother and his family must also die? When you sleep with a witch, you become a holder of their power. It won't make you a witch. It won't change the color of your eyes. But the next child you have may bear the mark. And if not that child, then his child. Don't be a fool, Kenar. When we start our holy war, there will be enough wealth for you to buy anything or anyone you want. But sleep with a witch, and you will be punished!"

"So that's why the entire family is listed," said Steven.

"Of course! Caster is no witch. Neither is his wife. But someone in his family, or hers, bore the mark. The proof was in the eyes of their dead son. Since we don't know which one passed the witch-power, they must both die."

"But that doesn't make sense," said the third man. "It's been over four hundred years since the rebellion, and who knows who slept with whom in all that time. Why, even you, Vincent, how do you know your great-grandfather didn't sleep . . ."

"Because I am a shaman!" Vincent shouted. "Because shamans know who their enemies are. Do you understand, Whily? We know!"

Whily looked at Vincent and suddenly became very quiet.

"All right," said Steven, breaking the strained silence that covered the campsite, "just don't forget when it's over, I want Caster's boat. Then maybe I'll be able to haul in a full net."

"When this is over, you will have whatever you want."

The three men with Vincent started to laugh. Seeing Kenar's face, and knowing what he wanted, made Susan feel as if worms were crawling inside her. She nudged Farrun, and after carefully turning around, he silently moved away. Susan followed, but as they crept away from the fire, she sniffed a small, feathery flower. Before she could stop herself, she sneezed.

"Silence!" Vincent yelled. Suddenly, he began a loud, monotonous chant. The sound rose up, covering the noises of the crackling fire with words Susan had never heard before. Though she couldn't understand the language, she understood their meaning. Vincent was calling her — ordering her to come into the light.

"Ne-for stu-me ohna eeno."

The words pulled at her like an invisible hand locked in a vise grip around her throat. Her mouth opened wide as she tried to force air into her lungs. Her feet froze and wouldn't move until her head faced the fire. Slowly, Susan's front legs turned and stepped forward. Even as her mind screamed *No!* her legs took another step toward the shaman standing next to the growing flames. Susan tried to turn away, to make her body obey, but it wouldn't. The feeble old man was forcing his will on her. The only thing

31

she could think of was the fire and the shrill voice that was reeling her in like a fisherman pulling up his catch.

"Ne-for stu-me ohna eeno!
Ne-for stu-me ohna eeno!"

Yes, thought Susan. *I am coming. I am coming.*

Farrun pushed against her, but she snapped at him. He would not prevent her from reaching her goal. Nothing would prevent her. She had to obey the shaman. She had to leave the darkness and enter the light.

Chapter 3

Just at that moment, Pern, the smaller moon that constantly revolved around its larger moon brother, Bern, passed directly between it and Reune. The mini-eclipse began to blacken the woods. Whatever moonlight trickled down was blocked by the thick layer of leaves, and the darkness hid the Susan-wolf. But the campfire flames steadily grew higher as they hungrily ate wood the men threw on. The firelight spread out as if single-handedly it could defeat the night. While the fire burned, Vincent repeated his strange chant, and as long as he called, Susan obeyed. She could see him clearly now, yelling his unknown words in a high-pitched whine, looking, trying to stare beyond the light. In a moment he would see her, and the green wolf eyes would give away her true power. She tried again to turn, but it was useless.

Then she heard it. The long, drawn-out howl of a hunting wolf. The cry stopped for the briefest of seconds before it began again. The next time Farrun screamed he was in a different location, and the dying echo of the first call met the beginning of the last. Farrun ran from place to place, howling at every stop. Kenar whirled, pulling a burning branch from the fire and swinging it in a wide arch. Steven and Whily jumped closer to the fire, hoping either its light or Vincent's spell would keep the wolves away. When Steven knocked into Vincent, the old man stumbled. His chanting stopped.

Instantly, Susan was free. She turned and fled into the night, panicked by a magic she had never heard of, a magic that had almost consumed her. She ran into the comforting darkness, but she did not run alone. Voices, old voices, ran with her.

"Run, Susan! Run!" her father whispered as he died.

"Where is she?" said a faceless soldier.

"Find her!" answered another man. "She'll bring a good price at the slave market and that will pay the dead man's tax. If we don't find her, the money will come from our pockets."

Susan was eight again, running, trying to cross the stream and find the hollow log she used for a hiding place. Her wolf's head looked left and right, but there was no stream — and until she found it, she could never be safe. The voices called, urging her on, faster and faster, farther and farther into the black-leafed forest. Suddenly, something plowed into her, knocking her sideways, slamming her into the trunk of the closest tree. She fell. Desperately, the Susan-wolf twisted, trying to get her four legs on the ground.

Farrun snarled and bared his teeth. He jumped, landed on her chest, and the Susan-wolf stopped struggling. She lay still, not moving, simply trying to breathe with Farrun's weight on her. Her heart slowed. The voices faded. She remembered who she was and concentrated on her real self. Suddenly, Farrun was sitting on a girl and immediately began licking her face while wagging his tail. She reached out toward Farrun's chest like a child trying to capture a bubble, softly, delicately. "It's . . . it's all right now," she whispered. "I'm fine."

Susan leaned against the bark of an ancient pine tree, gently stroking Farrun's fur, forcing it to lie flat against his skin. He, too, needed calming. "Thank you." Finally, Farrun lay down with his head across her lap. She continued petting him as she spoke. "No one ever told me there was magic in Reune. It frightened me, Farrun. Vincent called, and if it weren't for you, I'd be sitting by his fire now. Do you think the clan knows about the magic? The shamans don't come into the Thorals very often. And if the clan knows, why didn't someone tell me?"

Farrun made a soft, growling noise and bent his head closer to the hand Susan was using to scratch behind his ear. "I know, this is my testing period. If they told me everything I might as well have stayed home." After a long silence, she muttered more to herself than to Farrun, "I forgot what Maklin said. He told me never to be impatient and to think before I did anything. I didn't have to get that close to them. I didn't have to be afraid when Kenar said . . . they didn't know we were listening. I didn't think.

"I know," she said, answering Farrun's growl. "How could I have planned for that? How could I have even guessed that shamans can cast magic spells and force people to obey them?"

Farrun closed his eyes and leaned heavily into the scratch. He tried to growl, but it didn't come out right.

"Caster said something about magic; maybe I should have asked him? I shouldn't have felt that I was better or more powerful than Vincent, and I did. I assumed he was a harmless old man, and because I'm a Shape-Changer, there would be nothing he could do to me, especially in my wolf form. You don't have to tell me," she added when he yawned, "I won't assume anything anymore. And if I forget, you remind me."

Farrun sat up and licked her face. "You're right. Since Vincent didn't see me, we didn't make too much of a mess. Hearing you howl may have given away who we are. But if wolves live in these woods, then maybe he won't think of us. We're going to be more careful following him. Come on, let's go back to their camp. Only this time, we'll stay farther away."

The one shape Susan never liked to become was a bird. No matter how many times she practiced, she always felt uneasy seeing the ground from high up. Rillan had said that was because she was a wolf-child; she was rooted to the earth and would always feel lost when her feet had nothing to stand on. But today she had no choice.

The sun had just poked its head over the horizon when Vincent broke camp. He said nothing as the three men put their few belongings into their travel-packs and started off. They didn't even take time to cover the glowing embers.

Susan watched, hidden with Farrun under the bushes. After Vincent left, and before beginning her transformation, she smothered the coals with dirt.

Changing always took time, but the greater the size difference between Susan and the animal she would become, the longer it took. She sat perfectly still because this change was not easy. She wanted to become a rentia, a small, brown, sparrowlike bird that lived in all parts of Reune.

Instead of doing this in stages, like the fish, this had to be done in one motion. When she was ready, she began. In a slow, steady flow, her arms and legs pulled into her shrinking body. The arms bent crookedly at the elbows, skin sprouted feathers, feet became tiny claws, and two minutes after she started, a Susan-bird stood where only a Susan had sat.

A-NI-MAL-FLY! thought the Susan-bird's mind when she saw Farrun. Before Susan could react to the bird's instinct, the Susan-bird was in a tree branch.

Follow the animal. Follow Farrun.

Farrun began to run after Vincent, and the Susan-bird, flying from branch to branch, kept him in sight. *Not so high. Stay close to the ground.*

In a few moments, she saw the four men. Farrun held back and the Susan-bird continued branch hopping.

FLY-A-WAY-O-VER-TREE-MEN-MEN-FLY-A-WAY.

Again, before Susan could talk back to the bird part of her mind, the Susan-bird had flown above the trees. Susan almost panicked, seeing the ground move away from her so quickly. She would have closed her eyes except the bird part of her wouldn't let her. *No! Go lower . . . fly lower.* Slowly, the Susan-bird obeyed and flew behind Vincent and the three men, none of whom noticed a small rentia following.

After an hour's walk, the woods ended, and in a field beyond the last line of trees, the Susan-bird saw a small castle. As Vincent and the men walked straight toward it, the Susan-bird landed on the ground. She concentrated and became herself.

"I have to go into the castle," she said to Farrun, who had just joined her. "I need something small. What do you think?"

Farrun quickly jumped to his left and slammed his paw on the ground. Then he looked at her.

"That's not like you. That's more like a cat."

Farrun licked her.

"I know. You want me to become a mouse." Her only answer was a wet tongue across the face.

Susan looked into the sky to make sure nothing was flying near the castle — she didn't want to end up a meal for a hungry bird. When it was clear, she sat on the ground and concentrated. In a continuous movement, arms, legs, head, and body all became small and brown and mousy.

RUN-RUN-RUN!

No. Farrun won't hurt you. We don't have to run. As soon as the Susan-mouse calmed, she thought, *Go to the castle. Quickly, run to the castle.*

O-PEN-NO-GOOD-BIRDS-EAT-STAY-IN-TREES.

There are no birds. It will be safe. Go to the castle. Listen to me, go to the castle.

The Susan-mouse listened. It ran through the tall grass and if a hawk did fly by, it would never have seen the Susan-mouse. Farrun watched. Even he didn't see the tiny mouse run under the door and into the castle.

Susan let the mouse's instincts take over as it ran quickly from room to room. All she did was force it to keep going, looking for Vincent. Suddenly, the Susan-mouse froze as it turned a corner in a half-lit hallway. A large black-and-tan cat lay sleeping next to a closed door, and behind that door the Susan-mouse could hear Vincent's voice.

We have to go into the room.

NO-NO-CAT-EAT-NO-NO!

Susan looked. The cat was sleeping on its back, legs up, paws dangling, and head tilted to one side. Susan wanted to take a chance, to run for the door. On the other side of it, she heard Vincent again.

"What do you mean I have to wait! I am a full shaman, novice, do you understand that!"

Another voice answered. "Yes, Master Vincent. I am sorry, but Ometerer has instructed me to tell you he is very busy and will be with you shortly. You will have to wait."

The Susan-mouse heard a door close. She had time.

Run for the door. Run.

NO-NO-RUN-CAT-EAT-NO-RUN. The mouse part of the Susan-mouse would not move. The tiny animal remained in the darkened corner, motionless, except for an occasional twitch of her whiskers.

I have to do something! Think! That's when she remembered what she had told Farrun the night before, how Maklin had warned her many times not to be impatient and to think things out — to plan ahead. That's what she needed now, a plan. If she couldn't get the Susan-mouse to run past the cat, she had to either move the cat or find another way into the room. Since she didn't have time to find another way in, there was only one choice left. Now, how can a mouse move a cat?

The Susan-mouse searched the base of the wall in the

hallway and saw lots of cracks a mouse could hide in between the blocks of stone wall.

"Squeak!"

This time, it was the mouse-mind that could not react in time to stop the sound. Slowly, the cat's tail switched. It rolled over and lay on its side.

"Squeak!"

The cat yawned. Then, quicker than Susan would have thought possible, it charged.

The Susan-mouse ran and disappeared into the nearest crack. Deeper and deeper the Susan-mouse pushed herself. The cat meowed and stuck a sharp, curved claw into the space. The Susan-mouse squealed as her tail was pinned between the stone floor and the pointed claw. The cat pulled its paw back, trying to drag the mouse out. But all it did was cut the end of the tail.

The Susan-mouse ran several inches ahead. She wanted to turn and lick the cut, but when she heard the cat meow, heard its claw scrape against stone, she froze.

Go on! The cat can't get us.

But the Susan-mouse would not move. Her tiny heart beat wildly. The small pain in her tail was magnified ten times by the mouse-mind's fear. She knew she had almost been caught, and this place, dark and warm, was safe.

We have to go. Do you understand me? We have to go!

Slowly, reluctantly, the Susan-mouse obeyed. The Susan-mind had never realized how well mice can see in the dark; the Susan-mouse crawled the length of the stone easily, looked left and right, and scurried down the space on the wider left side. When it reached the end of that stone, the Susan-mind stopped it.

Go to the hall. Go to the hall.

The Susan-mouse obeyed and soon peeked into the corridor. The cat was still there, sitting next to the crack the Susan-mouse had gone into, slowly sliding its tail back and forth.

Run for the door, now. Run!

The Susan-mouse ran. The cat heard mouse feet on the stone floor and sprang after it. But the Susan-mouse was too quick. She ducked into the crack between the door and floor. As she turned and ran under a chair, the Susan-mouse heard the loud thud of the cat sliding into the closed door. Safe in her hiding place, all the Susan-mouse saw were feet — Vincent's and those of the three men with him. Just then, another door opened and a man wearing a white robe came out. His head was also shaved, but a lock of braided hair grew out of the left side, reaching the man's shoulder.

"My master will see you now," he said. The Susan-mouse ran after Vincent and the novice shaman as soon as they had disappeared into the next room. Once inside, she hid under a table. Though she could not see the people, she could hear them.

"You are?" said a deep, richly baritone voice.

"Vincent, Master."

"Yes," answered the voice again. The Susan-mind realized the voice must belong to Ometerer. "Vincent. I remember. You live in a fishing village, don't you?"

"Yes, Master," answered Vincent.

"You were involved in some trouble several years ago? The killing of a child before I had A'aster under control. Yes?"

41

"Yes, Master," Vincent whispered.

"Though I am pleased with your efforts to serve our order, sometimes it's best not to become too fanatical. When that happens, we lose sight of the greater picture. I hope you remember that, Vincent."

"Yes, Master."

"Good. But enough of the past. We have all made mistakes. Now, what brings you here? I have been discussing my plans with Lord Nieswim for removing Lord Falcon from his lands. I need his soldiers and we have only to agree on the price."

"Lord Falcon?" said Vincent.

"A green-eyed lord who lives in a northeastern province near the border. He has become too rich and too powerful. A'aster hesitates declaring him a witch because of it. But he will change his mind soon. Until he does, Lord Nieswim's private soldiers will follow my orders. I have decided to move to Falcon's estate, and Nieswim's men will take it for me. Falcon's family has been there for over three hundred years, and the house is . . . But that does not concern you.

"I am very busy, Vincent. Why are you here?"

Vincent began and told Ometerer what had happened from the time he recognized Susan as a witch until the night before when he had almost caught her.

"You interrupted me for that!" shouted Ometerer. "One green-eyed girl who you think may be a witch disturbs me from making my plans!" Ometerer pounded his fist on the table and threw his chair back as he quickly stood.

RUN-RUN-NOISE.

No! We are safe here. Stay here. No one will find us.

"Really, Vincent, you should grow a novice's braid again if following my orders is so difficult. How many times have you been told I want them alive? You know yourself our spells don't work all the time, and maybe, after I learn the witches' secret, we can prevent that from happening. How dare you order your villagers to kill the girl without my permission? How do you expect me to pry their secret out of them if you go around killing them before they have been properly questioned?" By now, Ometerer was almost screaming and Vincent began to inch away from him. "And another thing, how do you know that girl is a witch? Did you see her use any power?"

"How else could she have saved the boy?"

"Did you see her use any power!"

"No, Master Ometerer," said Vincent in a soft, meek voice.

"I thought so. Vincent, you are a bigger fool than I had imagined."

"But Master, Defender of the True Magic, she is a witch!"

"*May* be a witch, Vincent. Have you forgotten everything you were taught since I became head of our order? If everyone with green eyes had the power I think some of them do, we would have lost the rebellion four hundred years ago. Get this into your head — some of them are witches, Vincent, and that is why they must all be questioned before you or anyone else kills them. Do you understand that!"

"But I saw . . ."

Ometerer took a deep breath before he started speaking again. His voice was calm, but the icy chill in his words made the Susan-mouse move closer to the wall. "If you think she is a witch, then go and find her. And when you do, remember I want her questioned by the shamans I have trained. Then, and only then, can you kill her.

"Steeter," said Ometerer, "send an order to all the commanders of A'aster's army. Green-eyes are not to be turned over to just any shaman, but only to the shamans who have written authorization from me. Sign it 'By the order of A'aster, King of Reune.' Then, make a list of all those I have trained to question the captives and send them such authorization."

"At once, Master," said the novice who had brought Vincent into the room.

"But Master," said Vincent.

"Enough!" shouted Ometerer. "I have more important things to do than to argue with an incompetent! If you had not been in the order before I rose in our ranks, you would not be in it now. I am finished with you, and if you ever forget your orders again, you will be the one who is burned instead of this witch-girl of yours. Do you understand?"

"Yes, Master," whispered Vincent in a voice so low the Susan-mouse hardly heard.

"Good. Now get out of here."

The Susan-mouse ran under the first door and stopped in the crack under the second. The cat was gone. She ran along the edge of the wall, out the main door, and into the courtyard.

NO-NO-GO-STAY-HIDE.

It's all right. The grass is high outside the castle. It will

44

protect us. The birds won't see us. Go under the door. Go to the woods.

WOODS-SAFE. The Susan-mouse turned, scurried under the door, and headed for the woods.

Farrun sat up. He had been lying near a small, trickling stream when he heard the Susan-mouse walking on the dried leaves. He saw her coming and waited until she was herself before running to her, wagging his tail and licking her face.

"I missed you, too," Susan said, pushing him away and rubbing her rear end. "The next time you chase a cat, I might not yell at you. Come on, we've got to get away from here. Vincent will be coming after us." When they were far enough from the castle so Susan didn't have to worry about being seen, she told Farrun what she'd heard. When she mentioned Ometerer's plans about killing Lord Falcon, Farrun stopped and looked at her.

"No, I don't know if Falcon's one of us. No one ever mentioned his name to me. But remember, Ometerer said his family had lived there for ages. If he *is* clan, it's possible he's never been to the Thorals. Rillan said that sometimes clan members who decide to live outside our mountains teach green-eyed people they meet who they suspect have the power."

Farrun put his front paws far out as he pushed up with his hind legs. He yawned and sat.

"No, I don't know how they figure out who has the power without giving themselves away. But that doesn't matter. What matters is that Ometerer plans to destroy Falcon because the shaman wants the lord's house. What do you think about our warning him? We have to do something while we're on our testing time."

Farrun cocked his head sideways.

"No, I don't know where he lives. Ometerer just said in northeastern Reune, near the border. That means he's close to the Thundrous Mountains."

Farrun growled.

"I know those aren't the best directions, but at least it's a start. Well, what do you say?"

Farrun wagged his tail.

Susan returned to her wolf form. Before they started, the Susan-wolf waited while Farrun sniffed and licked her. When he was ready, they left. They backtracked through the woods, covering the distance they had traveled the day before. When they were past Lonis, far enough so that at the least Vincent would have to spend several days walking to reach where they were, Susan finally returned to her real self. She decided to walk as a girl rather than a wolf because she was worried about Vincent. She now knew that magic existed on Enstor, but she had no idea what it could do. When she asked Farrun if he thought Vincent could trail her by using that magic, he didn't answer. All he did was yelp once. Susan took off the travel-pack still tied to him, and he ran off looking for a meal.

Susan headed north, keeping the sea at her left. Falcon's land was somewhere far ahead and to the right. The problem she faced now was how to reach it. The quickest way was to stay close to the ocean. She could spend the next few weeks walking north before turning east, but if Vincent trailed her and guessed what direction she was going, that would be his path, too, since it was the easiest way. Another way would be to head northeast, crossing the woods and flat farmlands that spread out from the forest. But that way cut through the heart of Reune. There were hundreds of villages along the way, and Susan did not want to run into any shamans or king's soldiers.

The third way was the hardest. Susan and Farrun would have to march due east, through the woods and toward God's Hand Mountains. Not only would she and Farrun have to cross those mountains, but on the other side of them was a desertlike land that also had to be crossed. That land ended at the base of the Thundrous Mountains, a mountain range that marked Reune's eastern border. Then they could turn north and head for the province of Lord Falcon. Once they reached that point, Susan would have to find someone to ask for directions. It didn't take her long to decide. When Farrun returned, they began walking east, deeper into the forested hills and toward the mountains Susan couldn't see but knew were there.

"I've got to do something about this dress," she said later to Farrun as she stepped over several dead branches that had fallen across the path. "As long as I don't use my power, I'll have a hard time climbing. After you catch us supper, scout toward the north. There's got to be a village near here. See if you can sneak in and steal a pair of pants and a shirt hanging on someone's line."

Later that night, long after Farrun had disappeared, Susan sat tending her fire. She stared into the crackling yellow flames, and instead of seeing the burning white coals adding heat to the bottom of the fire, she saw images of the Thoral Mountains' white summer caps and heard Maklin's laugh as a younger Susan slid down the soft snow on a rough leather sled. Her hands tightened around her elbows, and her eyes half closed as she fought off sleep while waiting for Farrun. When she heard a horse softly approaching, she thought it was part of her dream.

"Vincent was sure you'd stay near the shore because that's the fastest way out of here, but after what happened in the forest last night, I got this notion you wouldn't want Vincent coming after you. So I borrowed a horse from Lord Nieswim's stable and rode this way. Once you reached God's Hand, no one would find you." Susan turned away from the fire and toward the voice. All she could see was a shadow. "I may not be a good fisherman," continued the voice, "but I know how to use this cross-bow. Besides, being this close, I couldn't miss. Don't try to run." The shadow stepped into the light.

First, Susan saw the sharp metal tip of the arrow as it rested in its wooden cradle. Next, she saw the arms that held the crossbow. She jumped up and took a step back when she finally saw the face of the man who owned those arms. *Kenar!*

Chapter 4

Susan swallowed hard. Instead of seeing Kenar as he neared the fire, she remembered the last time she saw his face, the last time she heard his laugh.

"I'm glad I found you," he said, throwing a rope at her feet. "Pick it up and tie it around your ankles. Then wrap it around your body."

Susan looked beyond him into the darkness, but couldn't see anything. A heavy layer of clouds prevented the moonlight from reaching the ground. *Farrun! Where are you?*

"You just sit by the fire while I make myself comfortable in this tree," he said after she had finished wrapping herself in the rope and he had tied up the end. "We're going to wait for that wolf of yours. Once he's dead, we can leave. I'm taking you to a deserted hunter's hut on the other side of these woods. Vincent will probably join us there in a few days, and if I'm lucky, Steven and Whily will never show up. That will give us enough time together."

Susan's mouth became dry, and she inched away from the fire.

"Don't move too far," he said. "I like looking at you. I suppose the wolf is out hunting. I hope he doesn't take too long. This isn't the most comfortable place to spend the night, especially when I could be sitting next to you."

Susan's heart raced. Both Rillan and Maklin had drilled her over and over in ways to defend herself when she couldn't use her power, but all she could think of was the tip of the arrow, all her mind heard was Kenar's voice saying again, ". . . time together." She swallowed noisily. Kenar laughed.

"Don't worry, little green-eyes. You won't be burned at the stake, at least not yet. Though it might be hard to convince Vincent of that, if he finds us. I've never seen him so angry. I heard Ometerer, the head shaman, yell at Vincent for bothering him. Ometerer called Vincent all sorts of nasty things and Vincent was really embarrassed. He's not going to get over it until you're dead. You know," said Kenar, starting to laugh, "if you really want to get even with him, when you die, make sure he doesn't find out. He's going to spend the rest of his life looking for you."

Susan's mind stopped working. Instead of trying to figure out how to escape, all she could think about was Farrun. *Farrun! If I keep him talking, Farrun will hear. If Farrun knows Kenar's here, then he'll save me.*

"Aren't . . . aren't you afraid?" she whispered.

"Don't be silly," he answered. "Why should I be afraid?"

"Vincent told you I was a witch."

"Vincent's an old fool. He's not even smart enough to realize that no power in Reune can do the things he claims you people can."

50

"But you follow him. Why?"

"Why not? You saw my village. As long as I stay there the best I can hope for is a full stomach. I want more from life than a net full of fish, and following the shaman is the only chance I'll have. In a few years, I'll be rich enough to buy anything I want. But that's enough talk. I wouldn't want your pet to hear me when he returns. Just sit there and be quiet."

Susan stared into the fire. The flames danced up and down, the wood popped and crackled. She moved her arms and felt the coarse rope holding them next to her side. Deeper and deeper the fire hypnotized her. She forgot the rope binding her, forgot Kenar sitting in the tree, forgot her lessons with Rillan about always controlling her power. *Change,* she thought without realizing it. *But Kenar's watching,* she answered herself. *Change anyway. That will save us. Change to what?* she half asked as the flames pulled her deeper and deeper into a trance. *I can't become a wolf . . . I'd still be trapped in the rope . . . the rope . . . something small . . . something that can hide in the rope . . . something like the rope . . .* Without Susan really willing it, she began to change.

In a silent, fluid motion, her arms, legs, neck, and head all contracted. Her skin turned scaly, her head pointy, her tongue forked. A snake-Susan curled up in the coil of the rope.

WARM-GOOD-WARM — NOISE — SOME-THING-COME-GO-GO.

The snake-Susan lifted her head; her tongue flicked in and out tasting the air.

HU-MAN-GO-QUICK-LY!

51

The snake-Susan began to push her way between the coils of the folded rope. Suddenly the rope was pulled up, and the snake-Susan was in the air facing a huge human. She struck — venomous fangs sank deep into soft flesh.

There was a scream, a long scream, and the snake-Susan was thrown over the fire into the woods.

NO-HURT-ME-BITE. But the scream faded and the snake-Susan remained still, hidden in the leaves. *COOL-WANT-WARM.*

The snake-Susan's tongue darted and smelled no enemy. Slowly, she crawled closer to the fire and coiled up next to a warm rock.

SLEEP.

NOISE-SOME-THING-COME-GO. The snake-Susan picked her head up. The fire was low, almost out. The clouds were still thick, hiding Pern and Bern, but the snake-Susan saw it. A large animal walking slowly toward her. The animal stopped several feet in front and sat. It stared at the snake-Susan but didn't move.

NO-LIKE-ME-GO.

The snake-Susan began to slide away when the animal got up and blocked her. Then it lowered its head and made a noise.

KNOW-THAT-KNOW-WHERE-WHERE?

Farrun?

WHAT-RUN?

Farrun . . . Farrun! Where am I? What am I? The Susan-snake began to remember. She concentrated on who she was — focused her eyes on her pet wolf — and let the power flow into her. She became Susan.

"Farrun!" But Farrun stayed where he was. When she

took a step toward him, he backed away.

Susan shivered, her shoulders and chest shaking violently. Slowly, she added more wood to the fire. When she saw Kenar's body, she quivered again, only this time it wasn't from the chill night air.

"Farrun, I . . . I . . . If you hadn't come, if you hadn't come . . . I would have been lost in the snake. I might never have become me again. I forgot my lessons. I forgot the things that Rillan drilled into me over and over. I changed in front of him. If he weren't . . . I should have kept control, Farrun. I told Maklin I wasn't ready. I told him."

Farrun sat and Susan saw his tail wag very slowly.

"I know you're angry. I know I shouldn't have let the power consume me. But it did and I'm going to learn from it. I won't let it happen again. I promise you, I won't let it happen."

Farrun took several steps and sniffed Kenar's body.

"I didn't mean to kill him. I never killed anyone before and you know it."

Farrun looked at Susan as she stood, not moving, near the fire. He remained still for a moment and then charged. Susan fell when heavy wolf paws hit her shoulders. Farrun licked her face as his tail rapidly moved from side to side. He jumped over her, lowering his front, raising his rear, as he continued to lick and make small growling noises. Susan could do nothing but rub his head and wait for him to finish. When he finally did, she wiped her face with the bottom of her dress.

By now, the fire was hot, and Susan sat close to it, pulling Farrun with her. "Ever since Rillan discovered I had the power, I've been learning. He told me what could happen if I wasn't careful, but nothing he said prepared me for losing myself like that. The scary part was when I was the snake, I didn't even know Susan existed."

Farrun closed his eyes and rested his head in her lap. He was being scratched in his favorite place, just above and behind his ears. As long as Susan continued scratching, whatever she said was fine with him.

"From now on, I'll try to do what Maklin told me to, think. Come on," she said, getting up. "I don't want to stay here anymore. Did you get the clothes?"

Farrun's head pointed and Susan followed his nose. There was a small bundle next to the horse Kenar had brought.

Susan went to it, holding up the shirt and pants she found. "The shirt's no good. It's been dyed. I can't shape-change in it. The pants are all right, though they will probably be a little big."

Farrun went to Kenar's body and pawed at his shirt. Susan shivered.

"I can't take that, but maybe . . ." She went to the horse and looked into the saddlebag. Inside, besides several journey cakes and strips of dried meat, she found another shirt of undyed wool. "I'll look silly with these oversized pants and shirt, but when we cross God's Hand Mountains, it will be easier than my dress." She stuffed the clothes into her travel-pack and tied that to the saddle, too.

"We may have to change our plans," she said as she put out the fire. "I'd like to keep the horse, though we'll never cross God's Hand with it; we'll decide later."

Though Susan's stomach still churned when she thought of Kenar, she was glad he had brought the horse. It was a well-cared-for mount and trotted sure-footedly over the hazy moonlit trail. The clouds were beginning to break and the light from the twin moons was getting brighter. They made good time, and by late morning on the next day, they reached the edge of the woods. Susan dismounted and walked the rest of the way with Farrun.

Somewhere far ahead, behind the dwindling fields, was God's Hand Mountains. North of them lay fields and fields of planted crops. This part of their trip would not be easy. When they had left the Thorals, the land was mainly untended and tall prairie grass had hidden them from view. This time, when they left the shelter of the trees there would be no hiding.

"We'll go straight east. When we reach the mountains, instead of crossing them, we'll ride along their edge. If we smell trouble, we can leave the horse and go on foot through the mountains."

Farrun shook his whole body as if he had just come out of a river. Then he trotted to the horse and lay down, curling himself up into a ball and tucking his nose neatly next to his tail.

"I guess you're right," Susan said, joining him. "It's been a long time since we've slept. But we can't oversleep. I want to travel at night as much as possible."

Farrun picked up his head and yawned loudly. Then he licked her face and went to sleep.

It was in the cool of late evening when they started out. They traveled a well-worn trail that wound its way between farm fields. Susan stopped once to see if whatever grew was ripe enough for her to steal. It wasn't. "When I finish the rest of Kenar's food, you'll have to hunt for both of us again," she said as she remounted.

They were lucky, and for the next few days were able to find secluded places to sleep the days away. At night, Farrun led her around the villages that dotted the countryside as they continued toward the mountains. On the fifth day, the pair left their hiding place early because Farrun smelled men upwind. They slowed when the outline of distant houses broke the monotonous landscape. Susan got off the horse and walked it through the fields, making a large circle around the nearby village. But as they approached the town, flames leaped up from behind the houses. The sudden light was followed by a long, drawn-out scream. When the scream died, a loud boisterous cheer replaced it. Susan froze. "Farrun," she whispered, "I don't like the sound of that. We've got to get away." Susan started trotting, holding the reins in a tight-fisted grip. They entered a field of chest-high corn and headed for the far end. Just then, they heard a second scream. The wolf growled. Someone was racing through the cornfield and not even trying to hide the noise. Farrun inched his front legs back and prepared to leap forward. When a second cheer rose from the village, the running feet sped up and broke through the last plants. A small boy skidded to a halt as a single voice speared through the dusk. "The child's escaped. Find him!"

The boy froze. Farrun stood and Susan looked into a fear-streaked face. Water-stained green eyes looked back at her.

"Come on! Quickly!" she urged, mounting the horse.

"Th–they'll . . . they'll ki–kill you, t–too, if they find you wi–with me!" he said, turning around.

"Farrun!"

The wolf jumped in front of the boy and forced him back.

"I said, come here," repeated Susan. When he stood next to her, she helped him scramble up. With the boy clinging to her, she kicked the horse into motion. Crashing through the corn, they came to a trail in seconds. Shouts chased after them and Susan knew they had been seen.

"Do they have any horses?" she said into the boy's ear.

"Lord Nie–Nie–swim's men are there. Th–they have."

Susan remembered the name. He was the lord Ometerer had been with. When she looked back, she saw several horses galloping after them. "We're in trouble, Farrun. There's no place to hide!"

He growled.

"Well, I didn't think of hiding in the field," she yelled back. "I thought about getting away. How was I supposed to know soldiers were there!"

Farrun remained silent. His muscles strained as he ran his fastest. Their only chance was to lose the approaching horsemen in the coming darkness, but even as Susan realized it, she knew it was a slim hope. The sun had set only minutes before, and though the moons had not yet risen, the racing horses would close the distance long before the darkness of night covered them. If she were alone, she could give up the horse and hide. But she couldn't; if the soldiers found the boy, they'd kill him.

Farrun was first to see it, a small walkway that must

have separated the cornfields of two farms. He turned into it, stopping suddenly when Susan followed. He snapped at her legs, telling her to get off the horse and giving her no chance to argue. As soon as her feet touched the soil, Susan pulled the boy off the saddle. She quickly turned the horse and slapped it hard on the rump. The horse ran through the field, away from the oncoming soldiers.

"You, boy, sit and don't make a sound. Farrun! Lead them away!"

Farrun took off after the horse. He would make sure it kept running, and in the dusk the soldiers might not notice no one was riding it.

Speeding hooves, sounding like a stampeding herd of cattle, charged down on them. Susan looked up. The dark shadows of night were slowly clawing their way toward them. If the soldiers hadn't seen her turn off the trail, she and the boy might make it. She ducked low, forcing the boy down. The horses came closer. Susan flattened herself, pinning the boy under her. The horses stopped. Susan held her breath.

"They've disappeared! They could be hiding anywhere in this field. Spread out!"

"No, wait! Hold your animals."

Susan recognized the voice. *Vincent! How could he have gotten here so fast? It's impossible!* She heard him mutter.

> "Me ha-da keynote eestar bremto,
> Me ha-da keynote eestar bremto."

"Is the boy in the field, shaman?" asked a voice.

"The spell should have . . ." Vincent stopped. When he

started speaking again, he was almost yelling. "How do you expect me to perform my magic with all the noise you're making! If you had listened to me before, the boy would be dead and we'd be looking for the witch-girl now."

"But we couldn't kill him. We have orders to . . ." started one of the soldiers.

Just then, her horse, with Farrun behind it, broke through the edge of the field, turned a corner in the trail, and vanished into the darkness. "There they are!" said one of the soldiers as Farrun howled.

Vincent's voice rose in a cracking scream. "It *is* the witch-girl. Follow the wolf! We'll get her now."

The horses leapt forward, leaving Susan and the boy alone. When he moved, trying to get up, she finally remembered to breathe. "Do you know the quickest way to God's Hand Mountains? If they follow, we can lose them there." She sat, holding his hand, keeping him close.

The boy nodded.

"The moons are late today," she said, looking at the sky. "In another few minutes, it will be black. Then we'll go. Farrun will keep the horse running, making the lord's men ride a long way. They'll have to wait until morning to backtrack and find our trail. By then we'll be in the mountains.

"Here," she said, pulling an ear of corn from the stalk. "It's not ripe, but it's all we've got."

The boy, rubbing his sleeve against his nose, took the corn and silently began husking it.

Chapter 5

The boy was a good guide, leading Susan on a twisting path that trampled no crops, making it difficult for anyone to follow. By the time the fields gave way to the rocky ground that formed the outer base of the mountains, they were far from the village. Susan stopped in the center of a large stream, cupped her hands together, and drank. "If we walk in the stream, it will make it harder to track us."

The boy looked at her. The twin moons had risen an hour ago and the light was bright enough to see. He nodded.

"My name's Susan."

The boy said nothing.

"Come on, I don't bite. What's your name?"

"Jef–Jeffrey."

"All right, Jeffrey," she said. "Let's go. Farrun, my pet wolf, will catch up soon. Don't be afraid of him. He won't hurt you."

Again Jeffrey nodded. After a few minutes of sloshing in the water, he turned and headed for the mountains. Susan was glad the ground was rocky because once the water dripping from their feet dried, they would leave no foot-prints.

"Wh–why are you do–do–doing this?" asked Jeffrey. "Th–they want me. If they ca–ca–catch you wi–with me, they wi–will ki–kill you."

"Why do they want to kill you?" asked Susan.

"Be–be–because m–my eyes. Th–they are gre–green."

Susan turned him around and the two faced each other. "I don't know if there's enough light, but if you look hard, you'll see that I have green eyes too. If that shaman chasing you catches me, he'll kill me. It doesn't matter if you are with me or not."

Jeffrey stepped back quickly and tripped over his feet. "Are you a wi–witch, too?"

Susan reached down to help him up, but he pulled away from her grip. "No, I'm not a witch. What makes you think I am?"

"Lord Nie–Nieswim so–sol–men said I–I was. Tha–that's why th–they ki–killed my . . ."

"Don't you believe that, Jeffrey!" She held him by the shoulders and wouldn't let go. "The shamans want to kill everyone with green eyes." They stood there, separated by the distance of Susan's arms. "I'm sorry about your parents."

Jeffrey wiped his eyes with his sleeve and Susan heard a muffled sob coming from him. "You m–may not be a wi–witch, b–but I am. I–I know where I ca–can hide. Sa–save yourself."

"You being a witch is about the dumbest . . ." She never finished because a dark shape bounded out of the night

61

and jumped on her. Farrun forced her down and ran around, sniffing, licking, rubbing his head against her and making small yelping sounds.

"Farrun," said Susan, trying to push him away, "we have to get out of here. Yes, I'm glad to see you, too." When Farrun was done, he looked at Jeffrey. "Farrun, this is Jeffrey."

Farrun stepped toward him and Jeffrey backed off.

"He won't hurt you, Jeffrey. Now, show me your hiding place."

"Please, I kn–know my way from here and can hi–hide in the mou–mountains. I've been there a–a lot. I cau–caused the dea–death of my . . . I do–don't want you to die for helping me."

"I told you before that the shamans are after me. One of them has wanted me dead since the first time he saw me. He's the shaman who ran after you in the field. Come on, it's time to go. I want to reach God's Hand before morning.

Jeffrey didn't move.

"As long as we stay together, Jeffrey," she said in a feathery whisper, "we're not alone. We have each other for company."

Jeffrey looked at his feet, and then back at her. "All–all right," he said, "but just un–until we get to the mou–mountains."

The night was quiet and Jeffrey said nothing as he ·walked next to Susan. She wanted to say something to make him feel better, but she didn't know what. *Maybe if I were older, maybe if I knew more about living . . .* But she soon realized that age had nothing to do with it. Maklin hadn't said anything that made her feel better after her birth parents died. *Maklin was right. Some things just can't be done.* So they walked on in silence. The moonlight made the jagged boulders take on nightmarish shapes and Jeffrey stepped closer to her as they walked under them.

The night dragged on — the twin moons slowly crept across a clear sky, lighting the way for the tired threesome. By the time they reached the edge of the mountains, Jeffrey leaned heavily on Susan; Susan's hand rested on Farrun's shoulder.

"There it is," said Jeffrey, yawning and pointing, "God's Hand."

She stopped. They were near the entrance of a small valley, tucked away between sharply rising hills. Though the moons were low in the western sky, it was bright enough to see the bleak landscape. All Susan saw was rocky slopes of naked earth pointing skyward.

The land appeared dry and dusty. Rocks carved into fantasy creatures by years of wind-blown sand were all that was there. Nothing, not even sturdy mountain grasses or shrubs, grew. "Look at this place," said Susan. "Nothing's alive here. Why would people call it 'God's Hand'? The land is dead. What god would have a hand in this?" They sat and Farrun laid his head on her lap; Jeffrey fell asleep.

Picking up a handful of soil and letting it drain through her open fingers, Susan whispered to her wolf. "I never knew what kind of mountain range this was, but I thought it would be like the Thorals, only not so high or wide. Look at those peaks. Half of them are straight up and down. I don't think even you could find a way across, and we can't leave Jeffrey. He would die here. That means we have to go north.

"I know," she said, answering Farrun's growl. "I don't like it either." She was silent for a minute as she looked over the dead land. "I've made a mess of things, haven't I? I didn't think things out when I saved the boy in the sea. Because I didn't, a shaman is chasing us. I forgot my lessons and killed a man. And now, we have to take care of Jeffrey until we find a place for him. I'm glad Maklin doesn't know what's happening. I don't think he'd like the way my testing period is going."

Farrun flipped on his side. He wanted her to rub his stomach. He growled once and when Susan began petting him, his head rolled, his tongue hung out, and his hind legs kicked out, pushing Jeffrey.

"I know. We've still got a long way to go before I return home. Things will get better. They just have to. I wish I knew what was ahead of us. If Nieswim's men were already in that village, who knows how many other villages they might have visited? We've got to get to Falcon's land quickly. I hope we can reach it without running into any more soldiers."

"It's–it's my fault," said Jeffrey, who had woken up and was watching them while his head was still on the ground.

"What's your fault?"

He sat up and began to pet Farrun. Susan guessed the wolf wasn't so menacing in the hazy predawn light. Farrun closed his eyes and twisted all the way on his back. He growled very slowly as his chest and stomach were being rubbed at the same time. Jeffrey had to speak a little louder when he started talking again. "The men who–who ki–killed . . . They're chasing you, too."

"I told you last night you had nothing to do with that. Vincent has been looking for me for days. The shamans think that just because we have green eyes we're witches. If they have their way, everyone in Reune with green eyes, or green-eyed relatives, will be killed. That's a lot of innocent people."

"But what if . . . wh–what if they're ri–right?"

Susan shook her head as she picked up another handful of dirt. She looked at him. He was smaller than she, maybe ten or eleven years old, with curly black hair and two large puffy cheeks. "How old are you, Jeffrey?"

"Twelve."

"Tell me, are you a witch?"

Jeffrey looked at her. His eyes glazed over and tears dripped from their sides. His arms and chest began to shake. His voice was barely a whisper. "I don't–I don't know. Yes . . . no . . . may–maybe. I'm dif–different. I–I can do things no one else can, things that fri–fri–frighten me, things that no one believes, things that are–aren't normal."

Susan draped an arm around him, pulling him close. Her voice sounded like a soft wind, barely touching his ears. "When I was little and my birth parents were still alive, my mother used to tell me fairy tales about elves who were supposed to have lived in our land ages ago and witches who lived then, too. The elves were good, and the witches were bad. When I think of a witch, I think of those fairy tale witches who were always evil. I told you what the sha-

65

mans believe about us. I told you that they are going around killing everyone with green eyes. That's evil, Jeffrey. Eyes don't make witches, actions do, and that makes the shamans more dangerous than anyone's eyes."

"But I . . . But I have done things . . ."

Susan stopped him. "What things?"

"I–I can't . . ."

Jeffrey's answer was cut off as Farrun quickly turned over and sat up. He sniffed the air and growled.

"They're coming!" said Susan. "But how, Farrun? How could they get here so fast? They couldn't have followed our tracks . . . they couldn't have!"

"Ge–get away from here, Su–Susan," stammered Jeffrey, standing up. "I–I know you're tr–trying to help, but it's no–no use. They're looking for me. I'm the witch they want. Please, lea–leave me alone." He turned and ran into the valley.

"Follow him!" she said to Farrun. "I want to see who's coming."

Farrun hesitated. He looked in the direction Jeffrey ran, then took one step toward Susan.

"Please, Farrun. I'll be careful. I have to see if Vincent is with them. I have to know how he managed to find us."

Farrun looked once more at Susan and ran after Jeffrey, while she crouched and waited behind a boulder. In the east, the sun's glow had just begun to brighten the horizon. In the west, Pern was making his last turn around his brother. Within a minute, the soldiers came into view. Susan counted eight, but what surprised her most was that Vincent wasn't with them. The lead rider stopped at the valley entrance long enough to wipe his brow with his sleeve. He looked into the valley, but when he saw nothing, he motioned for his men to continue. It wasn't light enough to see Jeffrey's and Farrun's tracks, and he had no patience to wait.

Susan waited until they were gone before getting up. But just as she was about to leave, she heard another horse and dove back behind the rock. In the growing dawn light, the last rider, bouncing on the saddle and holding on to the saddlehorn with both hands, came into view. *Vincent!* He was almost past her when suddenly he stopped. Susan dropped all the way down, pushing her back against the rock.

"No-trun-depor entay,"

she heard him say.

"No-trun-depor entay.

"It's working now," he muttered to himself. "Since we crossed that stream, my spell has been working. Stop, you fools!" he shouted after the soldiers. "This way!"

Susan heard the horse begin to run, and when Vincent's high-pitched voice faded into silence, she chased after Farrun. Maybe the three of them could climb out of the valley. She hoped so. If not, they would be trapped. It was easy following the boy and wolf. Once she entered the valley floor, the rocky ground gave way to powdery sand. Jeffrey ran straight, and on the windless valley floor, his footprints neatly pointed the way. What puzzled her was that there were more than one set of footprints — some led into the valley and some out. *Has Jeffrey been here before? I hope so.* Susan ran faster.

She heard Jeffrey before she saw him, yelling at Farrun, telling him to go away. Farrun, of course, wouldn't. When she reached them, they were at the back of the valley, where the two sides of the lifeless rock came together, keeping them prisoners on dead soil. "Why di–di–didn't you run a–away? Now they'll g–get you, too."

"Do you think I could hide in the rocks and watch them burn you?" she called back. "Is there another way out of here?"

"Why di–didn't you lis–listen to me? If my par–parents had listened to me th–they'd be ali–alive. They jo–joked about what I told them and when the sol–soldiers came, the peo–people called them witches, too. I'm–I'm not li–like you. I'm no–not li–like anyone else in the who–whole world! I want to die! Can't you understand that? I want to–to die!" His whole body shook like someone caught naked in a winter storm. "It's hap–hap–happening again, and I don't know how to st–stop it. Get away from me! I'll ki–kill you if you don't! Please! Please!" Jeffrey fell.

Dawn — the sun appeared, the twin moons lingered, Pern and Bern, pale globes in the western sky. Jeffrey's body began to shake. Susan stood planted to the ground as she watched Jeffrey's legs begin to shrink. His woolen pants melted into his skin and turned black. His legs thickened and his feet became paws. His chest collapsed into itself. Then the change stopped.

"He's a Shape-Changer!" whispered Susan. But Jeffrey had stopped changing. From the waist down, he was a panther with shiny black fur covered with even blacker spots.

But the rest of him was still a boy, a very frightened twelve-year-old boy.

His eyes darted back and forth. His animal legs kicked the air. His human hands clawed at the ground. "No!" he shouted, "Noooo!"

"Farrun, he's stuck in transition!"

Chapter 6

Both Susan and Farrun ran toward Jeffrey, but Farrun got there first. Just before he reached the boy, the wolf turned sharply, knocking his rear into Jeffrey's head. Though the force was not great enough to hurt him, it threw Jeffrey backward. The boy-panther lay still. By that time, Susan was there.

She lifted his chest and held his arms tightly as he struggled. *What can I say to him? I've never seen anyone stuck like this. How can I get him back? Why don't I know more? How could Rillan say I was ready!"*

Farrun pushed his head into her shoulders.

"All right, I'll do it. I have to do it." Susan continued to hold Jeffrey tightly as she began to rock slowly back and forth. Then, she whispered to him. "Jeffrey ... Jeffrey, relax. Think of yourself. Think of you the way you always are. No, don't open your eyes, just listen to my voice. Breathe deeply. Don't fight what has happened to you. Relax your body, think of yourself. You'll become all Jeffrey. I promise, you'll become yourself."

Jeffrey stopped struggling, his legs grew and returned to their natural shape.

"Listen to me, Jeffrey, I . . ."

Farrun growled. Dust from approaching horses rose into the air. The faint clop . . . clop . . . clops of horses' hooves became louder.

"Jeffrey," she said, getting up and pulling him with her. "I know what you are — and you're not a witch. I can explain everything to you but not now. Vincent is coming. You have to tell me where you were going to hide. You have to show us!"

"But . . ."

"Jeffrey, you must trust me! If you don't, we'll all be killed. Is there another way out of the valley?"

The boy didn't move. The sound of the horses grew louder.

"Jeffrey!"

Jeffrey ran to the end of the valley floor. "This way." He jumped onto a small ledge that was only a few feet wide and ended against the solid angle of the steep wall.

"Are you sure you know where you're going?"

Jeffrey pointed to the wall.

It was hard for her to see because years of erosion had worn the edges flush with the rocky wall. But when Susan brushed her hand against it, she felt a shape. Carved in the stone was the number "eight" lying on its side. There was something vaguely familiar about the sign, but Susan couldn't place it.

"Pu–put your finger in the middle, where the li–lines cross, and p–press," Jeffrey told her. Susan did it. First the rock resisted, but after a second her hand actually moved, pushing the rock in several inches. She turned to her left when she heard a scraping sound. A stone door hidden in

71

the mountain slid away, leaving a small, tunnel-like entrance in the rock.

"Hurry," said Jeffrey. "It'll sli–slide back in a minute and won't wor–work again for a wh–while."

She stepped in after Jeffrey and Farrun, just as the stone door sprang shut with a muted thud, leaving them all in total blackness. Air, cool and moist, greeted her. "It takes a few minutes for the light to come," whispered Jeffrey.

As they sat in the blackness of the cave, Susan felt for Jeffrey's hand and held it while she spoke. "How long have you known you can change like that?" Jeffrey didn't answer. "Listen to me, Jeffrey. You aren't a witch. You are a Shape-Changer, just like me. It means you have the power to change your body and make it look like any animal you choose. But that's the only power we have. We can't do magic. We can't recite spells as the shamans can. We can't stop the rain or make things appear or disappear. All we can do is change our shape. It's a power, Jeffrey, an old and special power."

Susan heard Jeffrey's breathing slow. She felt his hand relax in hers. "Are . . . are you sure?" he asked. "They said I wa–was . . ."

All of a sudden, the cave began to brighten. The light came from above without any sign of fire or flames. The ceiling just glowed all by itself. Susan looked down the lone corridor cut cleanly through the mountain. She wondered what this place was, but right now, she had to convince Jeffrey that he was not a witch. "Watch," she said, standing and moving away from him. Jeffrey's eyes and mouth opened wide as she quickly and smoothly used the

72

power to become the Susan-wolf. Farrun, who was still sitting next to Jeffrey, immediately went to her, wagging his tail. First, the Susan-wolf smelled and licked him. Then she walked over to Jeffrey.

He pulled his legs up and pushed his back farther against the wall. The Susan-wolf moved right next to him, poking her nose near his cheek. When she started to lick him, Farrun came and licked the same cheek, wetting both Jeffrey and the Susan-wolf at the same time. Jeffrey remained stiff for a moment, then started to laugh. He put his arms around both wolves. When that happened, the Susan-wolf backed up and became herself.

"Well," she said. "Do you still think you are the only one on Enstor who can do what you can?"

Jeffrey shook his head.

"Do you also believe me when I say we are not witches?"

"I . . . I guess so," he answered.

"Good," said Susan. "Now, tell me how you discovered you're a Shape-Changer."

Jeffrey remained quiet while he stretched his legs out and petted Farrun. Then, in a slow soft voice, he began.

"About a year a–ago, I dreamed I was a pan–panther. It was just a dream b–but when I woke up in the morning, I was–was here, in God's Hand Mountains." Susan noticed that as he spoke and continued to relax, his stuttering began to disappear. "I didn't know how I got here. But over the next sev–several months, I had the same dream again, and each time I dreamed it, I wo–woke up in these mountains."

73

"What did your parents say?"

"They told me I was sleepwalking and that m–my dream had nothing to do with it. They laughed when I told them about tur–turning into a panther. Then, about half a year ago, I had to ta–take a wagon-load of corn to another village. Two men grab–grabbed me, tied me up, and put me in the back of the wagon. They told m–me that after they sold the corn, they were going to take me to the sl–slave market. That's when it hap–pened."

"What did?"

"I don't know how I–I did it — all I kn–knew was that I–I wa–was–scar–scar–"

"It's all right, Jeffrey," said Susan, putting an arm around him. "You're safe, you know what you are, and as long as we're together, I'll protect you. We'll both protect you, won't we, Farrun."

Farrun raised his head from Jeffrey's lap, yawned, and put it back down, leaning into the hand that was scratching him.

"What happened then?"

"I turned into a panther and killed them! I re–remember running away after and hiding in some rocks. I must have fallen asleep because when I woke up I was me again. When I told my par–parents, they didn't believe me. So when the sha–shaman told me I was a wi–witch, I believed him."

"But now you know better, don't you?"

Jeffrey nodded his head.

"Later, I'll show you, *I hope,* how to control the power enough so you will only become your panther when you want to. But first, tell me about this place. What is it? How did you find it?"

"One day, after my dream, I woke up on the ledge. I guess it was just lu–lucky that I found the door."

Susan looked behind her. She knew she was leaning against a solid rock wall that hid the door, but it was impossible to see where the door ended and the wall began. It was all one solid slab. Looking up, she saw they were in the beginning of a tunnel neatly carved through the rock. She placed one hand on the wall. It was smooth, as if someone had spent hours grinding off all the sharp edges. When Susan looked deeper into the corridor she saw it curve.

"Come on," said Jeffrey, getting up, "let me show you. This is the cave's main br–branch. It goes off to the side several times, but this will take us through the whole mountain. I walked it once. There's another door at the far end, too. This place is mine. It's my secret and no one else in the whole world knows about it."

As they walked deeper into the cave, Susan not only wondered who had made it, but how and why it was built. Whenever she brushed the wall with her hand, it touched her with the same smoothness she had felt before. Just beyond the curve, the passage split like a "Y."

"The main branch stays to the left," said Jeffrey.

Susan saw how he knew. The side passage of the cave narrowed; the ceiling was lower, and the walls were closer together. Jeffrey turned into that passage and after walking several feet, pointed to a hole in the wall. Then he disappeared into it. "There must be at least a hundred rooms like this," he said, standing in the center of the rock-bound space.

Susan stopped at the entrance and looked into a large, square, empty room. "I don't understand," she whispered. "Are all the rooms like this?"

"All but two," Jeffrey answered, "and I can't get into one of them."

"I wish Maklin or Rillan were here. Maybe they'd know. Show me those two, Jeffrey."

He grabbed her hand and ran back to the split in the "Y," pulling her with him. "Wait until you see it. I even brought some stuff from home to fix it up 'cause it's my favorite place. Whenever I come here, that's where I stay."

Susan had to run to keep up with the boy because he wouldn't let go or slow down. He passed several other "Y" splits, but always stayed in the center passageway. He stopped when the wall vanished and an opening appeared. "You go first," he said, bouncing on his feet and grinning.

Susan peeked around the corner. Her mouth opened, but nothing came out.

"I told you this room was great," she heard.

Susan walked in. The room was smaller than the other one, but far more wonderful. In a corner, where the wall and ceiling met, there was a small hole. Water dripped from it. Her eyes followed the water down where it fell into a square hole cut deep into the floor. "A bathtub!" Susan said. When she moved into the room, she saw steps leading from the floor into the water. Farrun was there already, taking a long drink, his lapping sounds echoing off the walls.

"Look," said Jeffrey, walking around and kneeling at the edge of the pool. "See these holes? There are five of them on each side. The water runs into the holes so the t–tub never overflows. And see," he added, getting up and going to the other side of the room, "I brought some old cloth someone was going to throw out. I use it to d–dry myself. And look, soap."

Susan's mouth dropped open. "Soap! Jeffrey, I love you! I'm going to take a bath right now!" Jeffrey stared at his feet as his cheeks began to get red. Susan smiled. "I won't be long. Do you want to wait outside?"

Jeffrey nodded and left.

The water was clean, clear, and snow-runoff cold. It made shivers creep from Susan's wet toes all the way to her head. But she ignored the cold and walked unhesitatingly to the center of the little pool. Holding her breath, she ducked her head and let her hair float free on the surface. Then she took the soap and began washing. When she finished, she dried herself with one of the cloths Jeffrey had brought and put her dirty dress back on.

"I know," she said to Farrun, who was lying down near the pool, "but these are the only clothes I have. When the horse led the soldiers away, it carried my travel-pack with it." She called Jeffrey.

They sat together for a while, not talking, just listening to the water as it dripped from the ceiling. Susan broke the silence first.

"I was lucky," she said, making ripples in the pool with her fingers. "I was younger than you when my parents died. Maklin found me almost right after that and made me part of his family. It made the hurt of losing my parents a little easier. I can't say anything that will make you feel better about what happened, but I can tell you that if you want to go, there's a place for you in the Thoral Mountains."

"Ho–how would I get there?"

Susan laughed. "We'll take you. Only we can't take you now. You see, Jeffrey, I've just finished several years of training to use my power, and I'm on what we call a testing period. That means I have to spend time living on my own, making decisions, and trying to help the people I meet."

"You mean like me?"

"Yes," she said, pulling his hair slightly, "like you. Just don't expect too much of me because I'm not doing very well."

"You helped me."

"Sort of. I helped you get away from Vincent when you found us in the cornfield. But we were almost trapped in that valley, and if you hadn't have known about this cave, we would have been caught."

"I'm glad I found you, anyway. Where were you going when I met you?"

"Farrun and I are trying to reach a man called Lord Falcon. An army is about to attack his land and we want to warn him. I don't know what we're going to do after we find him. We'll decide that later."

"When you take me to the Thorals, wh–where would I live?"

"With us, silly. With Maklin and me and the rest of our family," she said, messing his hair up even more.

Jeffrey didn't answer right away. Then he nodded and

moved closer to her. "I'd like that."

"I wish I had clean clothes," she said, scratching herself.

"I never thought of that."

"Boys!" she said, shaking her head at Farrun. "Jeffrey, there are several things I have to try to teach you before we can leave. You have to learn to begin to control the power and I might just know enough to show you. We don't have any food, but if we let Farrun out at night, he can hunt for us. I don't know what magic Vincent uses to trail me, but I don't think he'll find this cave. When you open the door later, he should be gone. What do you say about staying here?"

"Whatever you want. Come on, let me show you the other thing I've found. Maybe you can figure it out." This time, Jeffrey didn't pull Susan, but walked next to her. He turned into a side passage, passed three empty rooms, and stopped. "There," he said. "It's the only room with a door. I can't figure out how to open it."

Susan dropped her arm from his shoulder when she saw it. Around the huge rock door were small oval paintings of animals. The colors and details of each picture made the animals look alive. She saw a zebra shining in its stripes, a leopard with tawny skin and black spots, and a large cat shaded with white, orange, and black bands along its tail. The animals' tiny green eyes seemed to stare at Susan as she stepped closer to the door. On its surface, Susan saw letters of an alphabet she didn't understand but recognized. She placed her fingertips against the stone and gently traced the words carved into the rock. She forgot about Jeffrey standing close to her, and whispered one word: "Elders!"

Chapter 7

Susan and Jeffrey sat on the floor, leaning against the wall opposite the door. They had already spent close to an hour inspecting it. Susan had seen the horizontal eight that was on the mountainside several times, along with words in the Elders' unknown alphabet. The two pushed every sign and every letter in the strange language, hoping that something they did would trigger a hidden key and open the door. But that only resulted in sore fingers. The painted green-eyed animals watched in silence; if they were part of the key to unlocking the door, they weren't telling.

"Who were the Elders?" Jeffrey finally asked.

"No one really knows. They were a race of people who possessed great knowledge and power. Many of us believe that we're their descendants."

"Do our green eyes tell us we have their power?"

"Don't let green eyes fool you. Not everyone with them has the power. But we think that's where it comes from. Maybe everyone who lived then was a Shape-Changer. I don't know. I think I know what to tell you so you can change into your panther when you want to. I just can't tell you why you can do it."

"How come?"

Susan chuckled as she remembered Rillan's answer when she had asked the same thing. "'Because some questions have no answers and that's one of them.' Anyway, legend says these Elders disappeared one day. They didn't slowly leave or die out. They simply vanished."

"Then how do you know they existed?"

"A Shape-Changer found a scroll a couple of hundred years ago. It was so yellowed and cracked it took forever to copy. No one knows what the scroll means, or even how to pronounce the words, because it was written in those letters. We're pretty sure the Elders wrote it because there were pictures of green-eyed people and animals on it. That's what was familiar to me when I traced the sign outside on the mountain door. You know what those letters mean?" she asked, pointing to the door. "This place was built by the Elders. Can you imagine what wonders might be behind that door?" Susan's whole body shook as chills raced along her back. "I can't wait until we find out what they left us."

"Us?"

"You said every room in this cave was empty. That means whatever is behind that door was left on purpose, and since we *are* the Elders' descendants, whatever they left belongs to the clan."

"But we can't get in."

"You're twelve and I'm sixteen," she said. "Maklin says part of growing up is learning what you can do and what you can't. The two of us can, I hope, warn Falcon that the shamans are coming, but we can't fight every shaman in Reune, and we can't get into that room. At least not now. But one day we might, and then we'll know what the Elders left behind. Let's go back to the tub room. It's time to begin your lesson.

"The first thing you have to know," she said when they had returned, "is that whenever you change, you must always wear undyed wool and plain leather shoes, like what you have on now. These will become part of you and reappear when you become yourself again. If you don't wear undyed wool, the panther will appear in your clothes and rip them. When you change back, you'll be naked."

Susan paused and took a deep breath before beginning again. *Don't mess this up. I can do this, I really can.* She closed her eyes and tried to remember what Rillan had said during their first lesson long ago. She listened a moment to the drip, drip, drip of the water, and when she was ready, she spoke slowly.

"Jeffrey, I want you to think of a huge farm field covered with layers of fresh white snow. Nothing in the world matters to you, nothing except that white field. In the middle of it, I want you to imagine your panther. I want you to see its rich, black, warm fur sitting on white snow. Close your eyes and imagine your body changing, turning into that panther."

Susan had to hold her breath because Jeffrey, even without her directions, had already begun to change. His arms and legs shrank — became thick and furry. His hands and feet — paws, his chest — oval and compact. Susan swallowed. *He has power! I never did it that quickly.* "Never stop concentrating, Jeffrey. Never let anything distract you from the time you start until you're completely the shape you want. This is the most important thing I can ever tell you because if you lose your concentration, you can become stuck like before, half Jeffrey, half panther."

Again, even before she told him how to progress, Jeffrey continued his transformation. His neck widened — his head grew, stretched — became new. The last thing was the tail — also thick and black, slowly sliding back and forth. The change was complete. Jeffrey was now a half-grown panther, but inside the sleek and powerful animal was the mind of a twelve-year-old.

If he can remember who he is, if he can keep his mind wholly Jeffrey, he will have done it! For a second time, Susan remembered to breathe.

A Jeffrey-panther sat listening to the lulling sound of dripping water, unaware that the power had obeyed him and molded his body into his new shape. Farrun stepped toward the Jeffrey-panther but stopped when Susan raised her hand. *Slowly now. This is important . . . most important. I have to make sure he remembers.*

"Go deeper into the panther," she said. "You are that majestic cat staring out at the world of whiteness. Yet when you look, you must see through Jeffrey's eyes, not the panther's. You must take from your panther its instincts, but you must give it your humanity. You must never forget that you are a human, a Shape-Changer, melding your body with your animal, taking from it its power and strength, and giving to it knowledge that comes from learning, not instinct. Never forget who you are, Jeffrey. Never. Now open your eyes."

The Jeffrey-panther blinked, shaking his head as if a pesky fly was buzzing in his ear. Susan knew why; he was seeing her from a panther's eyes. Jeffrey would have to get used to it. His head moved — sniffing and searching the room. When he saw Farrun, he hissed and crouched in one movement, ears back, hackles raised.

"Jeffrey is not afraid of Farrun. You're letting the panther tell you what to be afraid of. You must tell it. Do you understand? You control who you are, and you know there is nothing to fear."

The Jeffrey-panther stood. He stepped forward and then back. His teeth flashed, only to be quickly covered by a closing mouth. But they flashed again. Jeffrey was fighting himself.

Did I forget to tell him something? The panther-mind is trying to overpower the Jeffrey-mind. He's only twelve. Maybe I shouldn't have done this. No. He needs to know. "You can do it, Jeffrey. You can win. Think about who you are. Think."

The Jeffrey-panther turned to face the wolf. Slowly he stepped toward him. Farrun sat motionless, waiting. When they neared each other they poked their noses out. Susan heard it, a soft, rolling murmur that reminded her of waves near the Endless Sea. The panther was purring. He rubbed his head near Farrun's ear, marking the wolf as a friend. Susan ran to them, petting each with a different hand, while Jeffrey, still in panther form, licked her face with his long, rough cat's tongue.

"Good," said Susan after a moment. "Now, close your eyes again. Think of yourself. Imagine the opposite of before. Imagine your body stretching and becoming you again."

In a quick liquid motion that reminded her of Rillan's transformations, Jeffrey became himself. Susan sat, saying nothing.

"Did I do all right?" he asked.

Susan was silent for a while as she stared into Jeffrey's eyes. "You've done in one lesson what took me almost a week of practice. There's a power in you, Jeffrey, power that's greater than mine. You and your power are part of this secret cave, part of the Elders' hidden room. Something in that room called you and whatever it was, you heard. When that door is opened you must be the one who enters. You are the one the Elders want."

"Do you mean it?"

Susan laughed. "Yes, Clan-brother, I mean it."

Jeffrey's head snapped around to face her when he heard "Clan-brother." Silent tears appeared in his eyes. He reached over and hugged her. The tears became sobs — the sobs became cries.

"Cry, Jeffrey," she whispered, as they sat against the wall. "You have to get the tears out." Susan spoke quietly into his ear as she held him in a tight hug and stroked his hair. "I waited nearly a year to cry for my birth parents, and when I did, I cried for the longest time. Maklin started it when he cut up a rotted tree that had fallen during a summer storm. It reminded me of another tree, one I used as a secret hiding place when I was a child."

Susan's eyes watered as she rocked back and forth, holding him and remembering her own parents. Jeffrey cried, head nestled next to her shoulder. Then he slept. She stretched her legs and did the same.

Getting food was not as easy as Susan had thought it would be. When they woke, Jeffrey showed her the horizontal eight on the inside wall that opened the door. She was a little hesitant, knowing that Vincent might be in the area. But she also knew they had no choice. She opened the door and peeked out. It was late evening and only the dead land saw her. Farrun left and the door closed. When they opened the door an hour later, Farrun was lying on the ledge with a fat rabbit next to him. That's when Susan realized there was no wood in the cave to fuel a fire. They left the cave and walked far enough away from the dead land of God's Hand to find bushes and tree branches.

While Farrun scouted, they cooked and finished the last scrap of their meal. Under the light of the twin moons, and carrying as much wood as they could, they returned to the Elders' cave. But three times in the next few days they had to repeat their journey for more wood.

When they weren't doing that, they were in the tub room practicing. Jeffrey was a good student and was soon turning into his panther and back whenever Susan told him to.

On the second day, Susan became her wolf. After Farrun licked and sniffed her, jumped on her and rubbed his head against her side — a ritual he did every time — the Susan-wolf looked at a Jeffrey-panther. At first, the panther-Jeffrey hissed and backed away from the two wolves. But after the initial shock of seeing them, Jeffrey's mind took over. He walked to the Susan-wolf and began licking her with his raspy tongue. The Susan-wolf heard him purr loudly as he playfully bit her ear, then jumped over her when she turned her head to snap at him.

The three of them ran down the Elders' corridor playing tag or just chasing each other. Though Jeffrey was new to shape-changing, he soon mastered the panther's mind completely. The Jeffrey-panther was quick and agile, stopping and reversing directions before Farrun or the Susan-wolf could even turn their heads. Jeffrey took from the panther all the instincts that made it a hunter, but kept his mind in control.

Later that day, as they sat in the tub room and rested, Jeffrey asked Susan to teach him to become another animal.

"No," she said, shaking her head. "I don't know enough to teach you that. You got stuck in transition once and I was lucky to be able to get you out of it. But there's another reason. Remember the first time you became the panther? You had to control the panther's instinct to hiss at Farrun. You did that fine. But with any other shape, part of your mind always remains the animal's mind. Your mind becomes divided, half is the Jeffrey part, half is the animal part. The Jeffrey-mind has to constantly talk to the animal mind. While you're learning to do that, you must have a monitor, a person to watch you. I can't do that."

"How come that doesn't happen when I'm the panther?"

"Every Shape-Changer has a special animal, one form that is just as natural for that changer as being a human being. I am of the wolf; you are of the panther. When you are your panther, your mind never divides. You are Jeffrey and the panther at the same time."

"But you said I was good. You said yourself I have more power than you. Don't you think I'd be able to do it?"

Susan dipped her hand into the water and watched the ripples. "Listen carefully, Clan-brother. There is a danger every time you change. You can lose yourself, your human self, inside the animal. If that happens, you could spend the rest of your life as the animal, never remembering who you are. I know. It happened to me once and I killed someone. The Susan-animal didn't kill, the animal-Susan did. I lost control. I don't want that to happen to you; that's why you can't try it. Do you understand what I'm saying?"

Jeffrey hesitated a bit. "I . . . I think so."

"I want your promise, Clan-brother. You are never to try any other animal until you have a proper teacher."

Jeffrey looked at her and smiled. "All right, Clan-sister. I prom–promise."

He called me Clan-sister. I like it.

When they woke up on the fourth day, Susan decided it was time to leave. Jeffrey could change his form as easily as Susan, and Vincent, they hoped, was by now far away. It took several hours of brisk trotting, but a Jeffrey-panther, a Susan-wolf, and a real wolf finally reached the far end of the cave.

"I've only been here once," Jeffrey said, after becoming himself. "From where we entered God's Hand, the mountains go eastward, almost to the end of Reune. But the tunnel turned north near the entrance."

"So instead of going through the mountains, we went along their edge," she answered. "Lord Falcon's land must be somewhere ahead of us."

"How far?"

"I don't know. It could be a day's walk or a week's."

"What are we going to do after we've told him about the shamans?"

"I don't know that, either. We'll decide later. But, before we start for Falcon's land, I want to see what's ahead of us. I'm going to become a rentia, and I want you to wait here with Farrun. I'll be back as soon as I can. Do you know where the sign is on the outside wall? I want to be able to open the door when I get back."

Jeffrey nodded. "I'll show you. The door will close but I'll wait next to it until I can open it."

"Good. Farrun, you stay with Jeffrey."

Farrun jumped up and put his paws on her shoulders. He licked her several times and yelped once.

"I'll be careful." She kneeled down and kissed his big, wet nose. "You know how I feel about being a bird, so believe me, I'll be careful!"

Chapter 8

Standing just outside the cave with Jeffrey watching, Susan stood still and concentrated. At first, it was difficult because Jeffrey sat, elbows on knees, chin in hands, eyes at their widest. As soon as Susan began to change, he oohed and aahed, and the sounds, along with his amazed expression, broke her concentration.

Concentrate! One Clan-brother as an audience shouldn't make a difference. But it did and she had to start over three times before the Susan-rentia stood on the ground.

HU-MAN-A-NI-MAL-FLY-FLY.

The Susan-rentia left the bird's instincts alone until they were airborne. But almost immediately afterward, she fought for control. *Not so high! Fly lower, fly lower.*

NO-LOW.

Yes, low! And turn north, away from the mountains.

NO-NEED-ROCK-TO-HIDE-MOUN-TAIN-SAFE.

Susan thought to the bird's mind again, but it was no use. The Susan-bird continued into the mountains south of Jeffrey, who was watching from below.

Think. Think! Then she got an idea. *Fly high. Fly north,* she offered as a compromise to the rentia's mind. *We'll look for food, water, and other rocks to hide in.*

HIGH-NORTH, the rentia's mind thought back. The Susan-rentia quickly rose several hundred feet into the air and made a sharp U-turn. Her human stomach would have felt sick, but the Susan-human had no stomach now, and the Susan-rentia's stomach was used to flying. But knowing that didn't make the Susan part of the rentia's mind feel any better.

The Susan-rentia flew northward. It was a clear summer's day and nothing, not even a hint of a cloud, blocked the sun or her vision. To her right, the land grew gradually dry. The farms petered out, leaving only short, tough shrubs. They were part of the desert that stretched east until it reached the beginning of the Thundrous Mountains marking the end of Reune. The Susan-rentia veered into the desert land, looking for signs of life that could either threaten or help them if they went that way. She saw only dry earth.

She turned, flying more west than north. The farther west she flew, the busier the land. Farmers plowed and fields of leafy green crops grew. *Lower. We have to fly lower.*

NO-LOW-ER-MEN-STAY-HIGH.

Susan didn't argue this time. By now, she was almost, though not quite, used to flying two hundred feet above the surface, and she was heading in the direction she wanted to go. After passing an apple orchard of carefully tended trees, she saw a small village and rested on the top of one of the huts. The bird's mind took control and dove for a small birdbath someone had placed on a shaded rock. Again, it took the Susan part of the bird's mind a moment to recover. As the Susan-rentia drank and splashed water over herself with her wings, she noticed soldiers grooming horses with flowing manes. The men were relaxed, talking quietly among themselves. If they planned to fight, their enemy was far away. If they had already fought, they had no wounds to show for it.

Then the Susan-rentia flapped its wings. Two men with shining bald heads and long white robes had left one of the huts. The Susan-bird flew. In a moment, she had left the village and was over farmers bending their backs and pulling weeds from their fields. Susan thought about the shamans. They were like those farmers, ridding the land of her people. But unlike the farmers, who discarded only the weeds, the shamans destroyed everyone they didn't like or anyone who had something they wanted. If only they didn't possess some kind of magic, then maybe they wouldn't be so powerful. If only she could discover what that magic was and figure out how to fight it.

It's hard to think of two things at once, and thinking about the shamans' magic made her concentration waver. The Susan-rentia fell from the sky. Not all the way, but far enough to make Susan stop worrying about magic she could do nothing about. Flapping wings and the rising hot air brought her to tree height on the treeless plain.

HIGH-ER.

No, answered Susan's mind. *No.* This time, she won. She quickly flew north, the only direction she could take with Jeffrey. Soon, the land began to have features other than flatness. Tiny hills with green-brown bushes appeared. Next a river, or at least a large stream coming from the north, made a sharp turn and pointed to the sea far to the west. Finally, she saw cows and horses lazily shooing flies with their tails in pastures surrounded by low, full-leafed trees. Though she looked, the Susan-rentia saw no people. Then she saw the dark clouds. *No, not clouds, smoke.* She flew higher. What should have been a village was charred debris with vultures fighting over the dead.

Suddenly the Susan-rentia fell for a second time. The bird's instincts took over and she flapped her wings frantically, but it wasn't enough to prevent the Susan-rentia from hitting the ground. Faster than she would have liked, Susan became herself. *All those bodies!* The vultures fighting over the remains of the villagers made her stomach churn. She tried to become her rentia again, but it was impossible to concentrate, hearing the bickering vultures. She shivered in the summer heat and walked away. If this was the beginning of Falcon's land, it was too late for her message. If it wasn't, she wondered why the village had been destroyed.

Twenty minutes later, when the village was a small dot behind her, Susan had calmed. She became a rentia again and flew back to the cave. It was getting late and she was tired. She wanted to feel Farrun's licks on her face and her new clan-brother's hand in hers. But most of all, she wanted to forget the burned village; the smoking huts reminded her of another smoldering house.

An hour after she returned to the cave, the three set out. Though it was late afternoon, Susan wanted to reach Falcon's land as soon as possible. They traveled north, stopping in the early evening and waiting for Farrun to catch their dinner.

"Did you find Falcon's land?" asked Jeffrey.

Susan shook her head. "No. I'll tell you everything to-morrow. I just want to sleep now." She curled up near the fire, and as soon as her eyes closed, it was morning.

When she awoke, Susan told the boy what she had seen. "We have to avoid the village with the shamans, and pass the burned-out one."

"Why don't we become our animals?" asked Jeffrey. "We could go much faster."

Susan thought for a while before she answered, remembering a story Maklin had once told her. "Tell me, Clan-brother, where would you hide a special tree?"

"What?"

"Think about it."

"I don't know. Where?"

"In a forest, Jeffrey. In a forest with hundreds of other trees. Do you understand?"

"No."

Susan put an arm around him, pulling him closer. "Wolves and panthers live in the forests and mountains of Reune. There are no forests here. And wolves and panthers don't travel together."

"But Farrun's with us."

"Yes," answered Susan, reaching down with her other hand to pet the wolf, "he is. But he's with two humans, and though a wolf is not a normal pet, it's not unheard of. When you become your panther, and later when you learn to become other animals, you must always blend in with your surroundings so you won't stick out. Now do you understand the story about the tree?"

"I think so."

For two days they walked. Crossing a small stream, they

heard the sound of a trumpet blowing in front of them.

"What's that?" said Jeffrey.

Farrun ran forward about a hundred feet and sniffed the air. Then he turned his head to Susan and growled. Susan shaded her eyes with her hand, but couldn't see anything. The ground was just beginning to change from semiarid waste to almost usable farmland; far in the distance, Susan could see the brown ground cover give way to green.

"Listen, Jeffrey. We're going to change. Stay with me and change back as soon as I do. All right?" When Jeffrey nodded, she called to Farrun. "No playing this time, understand?"

Susan began. Jeffrey changed faster than she and was already his panther by the time a Susan-wolf stood on four legs. Three animals raced toward green growth and trumpet's blare, and when they reached the beginning of the field, two became human. Now boy, girl, and wolf ran. They reached the field's end — a trumpet blew a second time. Susan dropped down and pulled Jeffrey with her. What they saw was a strange sight.

Off to their right was a large group of riders, twenty-five or thirty men. Though the horses' necks rose and fell as they pulled up clumps of yellow grass, the men on them sat like motionless statues. On the left side, there were more riders. Those men were not frozen. However, they moved as if they were trapped in mud. Their swords waved slowly in the air, and they could not kick their horses hard enough to get the animals to charge.

Several hundred yards ahead of both groups of riders was a company of king's soldiers. They were approaching slowly, staying about a dozen feet behind two shamans, also on horseback. Those shamans, one facing the rigid men and one facing the slow-moving men, were shouting.

"In no lu-ter!
In no lu-ter!"

Instantly Susan's body became stiff as wood. Obviously, one shaman was having a problem casting his spell. But the shaman closest to Susan and Jeffrey wasn't. Susan couldn't move even her little finger.

"Su–Su–" she heard. "I ca–ca–"

What's happening! What are they doing? Who are these shamans?

Suddenly, Susan saw movement. The shamans' magic had no effect on animals and Farrun was running. *Faster, Farrun, faster!* Susan hoped the soldiers would not see him until he attacked. When Farrun was almost on top of the two shouting men in white, the wolf leaped. Lowering his head and biting the first man on his neck, the two began to fall. Blood raced down the shaman's shoulders only to be soaked up by the white robe. Farrun let go, kicking out with his hind legs to push off against the shaman's horse. He twisted in the air, getting close enough to the second shaman to bite his arm. His teeth clamped tight — man and wolf tumbled. When they hit the ground, Farrun turned and viciously tore open the shaman's throat.

Instantly, the spell was broken; the men who had been enchanted charged. When the shamans died, the king's soldiers must have lost their confidence. The fight was short and brief. Within minutes, the soldiers still alive ran away.

While the battle was being fought, Farrun returned to Susan. He stood in front of her and Jeffrey, hackles up, teeth bared, growling in a low constant voice, making sure no horse or rider came near.

Jeffrey buried his head in Susan's shoulder. "Wh–what ha–hap–happened? I wa–was fri–frightened."

"I don't know," whispered Susan.

When the fight was over, the men who had won re-grouped. Several of them collected knives and swords of the dead as one man rode toward Susan.

Farrun, his chest still red, growled loudly, inching his front legs back, ready to jump. But the man stopped. Though his hands and face were smeared with blood, Susan saw a neatly trimmed white beard covering his cheeks. The man was not overpoweringly large, but then again, he wasn't short. He dismounted, unbuckled his sword, and laid it across his saddle.

He wiped his face with the back of a hand and Susan saw wrinkled and loose skin along the sides of his arms. Then he rubbed both palms over the stiff leather vest he wore. He waited until Farrun's growling became quieter before slowly stepping toward the wolf. That's when Susan and Jeffrey stood up. The man looked at her. His head nodded, a smile crossed his lips. Susan thought she knew why. Emerald-green eyes were watching her and Jeffrey.

When the man was only an arm's length from Farrun, he kneeled. He extended his hands out and let Farrun, who was still snarling, smell them. After a moment, Farrun trot-ted back to Susan.

"Thank you," he said to the three of them. "The shamans' spell works only as long as it's chanted. The wolf saved our lives. Tell me, who are you? Why are you here?"

"I'm Susan Terance," she said, "and this is Jeffrey."

"Where are you from?" he asked.

"I'm from Li–Lief," answered Jeffrey. "It's a far–farming . . ."

"I know where it is," said the man softly. "And you?"

"The Thoral Mountains."

"The Thorals! You're not going back to where you were born, are you? You're not obeying Ometerer's edict?"

"No," answered Susan. "We're looking for a man named Lord Falcon. We want to warn him that Ometerer wants his land."

"I am Lord Falcon, Susan, and I know. Now listen, because I can't talk here. Are you clan?"

That was the one question Susan had never expected to hear. Even the non-clan people who lived in the Thorals and probably suspected something of the clan's power never asked openly.

"Susan," said Falcon, "we don't have the time to discuss it. It's dangerous here. Is this your testing?" When Susan nodded, Lord Falcon shook his head. "It's a stupid time for it. The whole country's going crazy now that that lunatic Ometerer is in charge."

"But King . . ." started Susan.

"Not now," said Falcon, interrupting. He pressed two fingers of his left hand to his lips and whistled. One of the men left the group and rode toward them. "I need two horses and several days' rations," he shouted. "Susan, you and Jeffrey ride north until you come to what was once the village of Tysor. When you reach it, turn east. After several hours, you'll begin to see mountains in the distance. Those are the Thundrous. Keep going until you see two very tall twin peaks slightly to the north. You can't miss them. Ride straight for those peaks. About half a day from when you see them, you'll come to a forest. I want you to be at least a mile or two inside the forest before you camp. Wait there. Someone will come for you and take you to my manor. I'll join you as soon as I can."

"All right," said Susan.

"It should take you a couple of days. Ride as quickly as you can. Reune is going mad and none of us," he paused, looking at Susan and Jeffrey, "is safe."

By now, the man had returned with two horses and Lord Falcon gave their reins to Susan and Jeffrey. "There are only journey cakes here," he said, "so the wolf will have to go hungry until you reach the forest. He can hunt there. But don't let him leave you until you reach the trees." Lord Falcon didn't wait for an answer. He turned, mounted, and called for his men to follow as he rode off. Within minutes, Susan, Jeffrey, and Farrun were all alone except for the dead bodies and the vultures beginning to circle high above them.

Chapter 9

Susan did what Falcon asked. She and Jeffrey headed toward the forest, walking when the horses were tired, and
riding at a gallop when they weren't. Farrun scouted, and
for once, luck was with them. No one bothered them as
they rode north. The few farmers they saw in the distance
did no more than throw them a passing glance.

"Something has to be very wrong," said Jeffrey as they
skirted a large field. "Where is everybody? There were
only a few people in that last field. The crops won't grow if
they aren't tended. A lot of people are going to be hun–
hungry this winter. I know. When the crops didn't do well
in Lief, ev–everyone went hun–hungry." When he mentioned the word "Lief," he became quiet and rubbed his
eyes with his hands.

Susan didn't answer. There was nothing she could say.

"Look!" said Susan, pointing. They had passed the
burned village almost six hours ago and Susan was beginning to worry that they were not going in the right direction. But there, far in the eastern horizon, was the shadow
of the Thundrous Mountains. "They're bigger and taller
than the Thorals," she said. "You know, there are four dif-

ferent countries on the other side of them. I remember that from Rillan's lessons. I wonder if any clan lives there?"

After riding toward the mountains for another few hours, they saw the twin peaks that Falcon had told them about. The top of each peak was glistening white, and as sweat dripped down Susan's neck, she became homesick. "It can't be long now. I'll be glad when we find the forest. Farrun will be, too. He's hungry!"

"You and he won't be the only ones," Jeffrey said, lifting himself up and rubbing his behind. "I hurt from riding this long." But they rode the rest of that day without coming close to the woods. Near noon on the following day they finally saw it.

Farrun howled, running ahead and waiting near the edge of the trees. Susan heard an answering howl coming from the woods they were rapidly approaching. "Farrun has company. Go ahead, Farrun. We'll be safe for a little while. Find something to eat." Farrun looked at her, then ran off as Susan and Jeffrey entered the cooling shadows.

"Now where?" asked Jeffrey.

Susan saw a small path. "We'll take that for a while. I just hope that whoever is supposed to come for us doesn't take too long. I'd like to take a bath and have something good to eat."

The small road snaked its way through thick columns of trees, and Susan saw the way Jeffrey stared up at them. "The Thorals have forests like this. Some of them have pine trees twice as high, and each one has a hundred arms spreading out like this." She opened her arms wide and spread her fingers as far as they'd go. "The earth under

101

those trees has forgotten what sun looks like. I've spent hours walking there. Wait until you see those forests, Jeffrey, wait till you see them."

But Jeffrey was awed by this forest. "These are bi–big enough. We don't have trees in Lief and the tallest things I've ever seen grow is corn. This place is fa–fan–fantastic!"

Susan smiled to herself as she watched him look upward, seeing the bottoms of countless leaves, and only tiny slivers of sunlight that found a way through the branches to touch the ground. There was an eerie silence about them as they rode.

"Are forests always this quiet? I don't hear anything but our horses."

"Whatever animals there are probably hear them, too. That's why you don't hear any animals." They rode in that silence, moving from dark shadows to lighter ones. Susan didn't speak, knowing that any sound would break the spell the forest was casting over Jeffrey.

They came to a small clearing and made camp. By the time the fire was hot, Farrun had returned with a rabbit. He dropped it and bounded for Susan, licking and wagging his tail. Then he went to Jeffrey and put his head in the boy's lap. He growled softly; he wanted his head scratched.

"He's a smart one," said Susan, laughing. "He knows I have to prepare the rabbit and can't scratch him while I do."

"You and Farrun stay here," she said after they had finished eating. "I want to see where the path leads."

"But Lord Falcon said to stay..."

"Falcon told us to wait until someone comes," she answered. "But he didn't say I couldn't peek."

Farrun growled at the same time he wagged his tail.

"I'll be careful," she said. "I promise."

She closed her eyes, and ignoring Jeffrey's oohs and aahs, became her rentia.

FLY-FLY-A-NI-MAL-DAN-GER-FLY.

Susan didn't talk back to the rentia's mind and let the bird fly up and land on the top of a nearby tree. Far ahead, the Susan-rentia saw two spiral towers. *That must be the manor.*

It took several minutes to reach the house because instead of flying directly, the Susan-rentia flew from tree to tree. *It's beautiful!* It was a long, two-level house, built completely of whole logs cut from the surrounding woods. The logs fit snugly on top of each other and their ends were cut evenly. The towers she saw were attached to two ends of the building, and in each was a man watching the land.

Beyond the house, she saw fields of corn and other crops, and far in the distance the beginnings of the Thundrous Mountains. *They are like the Thorals.* Where the mountain peaks poked high into the sky they were capped in white, and when they were low they were layered with pine green. *Now these ARE mountains! Jeffrey must see this.*

No one came for them that night, and Susan built up the fire just before going to sleep. Off in the distance, she heard the sounds of wolves calling to each other. Though

Farrun poked his head up once or twice, he ignored his real brothers. He was content to sit by the fire and be scratched by either Susan or Jeffrey or both.

In the morning, Farrun's loud growl woke the two. They stood next to the wolf, facing the path Susan knew led to the manor. Soon, a single rider appeared. "You're up early," said the horseman.

"Who are you?" asked Susan.

"You're the ones who are trespassing," he answered. "but I didn't ask who you were."

"Lord Falcon told us to meet him at his manor," said Susan.

"Then I suspect it would be best if you came with me," he answered. "You'll never get there by staying here."

"How do we know you're from Lord Falcon?"

The man shook his head. "Suspicious young lady, aren't you?" He laughed to himself as he pulled his sword and quickly reversed it, carefully holding the blade. He moved his horse next to Susan. "Take my sword. When you're satisfied I'm the Lord's man, give it back to me. Until then, he'll protect you," he said, looking at Farrun. He held the sword out, hilt first.

"I guess it's all right," Susan said, refusing to take the sword.

"I guess it is," answered the man as he chuckled again. "Come on."

"Just a second," said Susan. Before she mounted, she made sure the fire was completely out and the ashes were covered under the forest dirt.

"Are you alone?" asked Jeffrey.

Again the man nodded. "Someone's been watching you

since early last night," he answered. "These days, it's best not to trust anyone until you've made sure they are what they say they are. Your young lady-friend has figured that out."

"Wh–who was here? Even Farrun didn't know."

But the man didn't answer. Instead, he just turned his horse and walked away.

It took several hours to reach the manor, and the man dropped them off next to the front door. Almost as soon as he left with their horses, the door opened.

"Wow!" whispered Susan. "This place is gorgeous." The furniture she saw was highly polished wood ranging in shades from mahogany red to oak brown. Tapestries showing mountain scenes and a variety of animals, both wild and tame, hung on the walls. There were rugs on the floor, plants growing under the southern windows, and shiny wood-floored halls. The sound of Farrun's nails clicked on the floors until Susan nudged him onto the long runner rugs their guide walked on. The elderly woman who had opened the door and led the way stopped at a closed door.

"You children must be hungry after that long ride. Letting you spend the night in the woods probably didn't do you any good, either. But we have to be careful nowadays. Go eat, and when you finish, there'll be hot baths for both of you."

"Baths!" said Susan. The old woman smiled and opened the door.

Jeffrey rushed past Susan. "I'm hungry." Breakfast was hot steamy porridge that tasted as good as it smelled, freshly baked bread, and wedges of cheese and fruit. The woman came back carrying a large bowl that she put in front of Farrun.

"You have to eat, too," she said, stroking him twice on the head. "That's fresh milk and meat left over from yesterday's dinner."

The wolf poked his nose in the bowl, noisily lapping up the milk and swallowing the meat floating in it.

When they had finished a girl not much older than Susan appeared. "If you'll come with me, I'll show you to your rooms." The first room she went to was on the second floor. It was large and its windows faced the far mountains. "This will be your room," she said to Susan.

"Can I stay here, too?" asked Jeffrey.

"Sure," the girl answered. "I'll have another bed brought in."

"Thank you, er . . ."

"Nancy."

"Nancy, I'm Susan and this is Jeffrey."

"The bathing room is the second door on the right. Why don't you go first," she said to Susan. "I'll get fresh water for Jeffrey afterward."

"I'm not that dirty," protested Jeffrey.

"Yes he is, yes he will, and thank you again. Boys!" she said to Farrun when Nancy had left.

The tub was large, the water hot. Susan must have spent close to an hour just soaking after she washed herself. Several times, Nancy came in and carefully poured more hot water into the tub. When Susan finally went back to her room, she found Jeffrey sleeping on the second bed, dirty clothes and all. She woke him up, pointing to the hallway.

Nancy came in a minute later and held an undyed woolen dress and a soft pair of leather boots. "I hope these fit. They won't even use your dress for rags." When Jeffrey finally came in, he, too, was wearing new clothes.

"Look," she said to him, pointing to the mountains out the window. "Those are like the Thorals. If you liked the forest we came through, wait until you see those close up!"

They went downstairs and asked a man they saw when Lord Falcon would return. He said he didn't know. No one else knew either. When they saw the woman who had let them in, Susan spoke to her. "Is there anything we can do to help while we wait for Lord Falcon?"

The woman just shook her head. "You don't have to do anything, child. I have a feeling that when my lord returns, we'll all be very busy. Just enjoy yourself."

So they did, and for several days, the pair did nothing but eat or sleep, or take walks in the woods with Farrun.

"I could get used to this," said Jeffrey as they lay in their beds at night.

"Don't get spoiled. Once we leave, it will be a long time before we get treated like this again. We don't even live this well in the Thoral Mountains."

"Well, I haven't heard you complaining very loudly," he said. Before Susan could answer, a pillow hit her in the face. Her pillow flew right back, knocking Jeffrey off his bed. That started the two of them swinging pillows wildly at each other. Farrun watched for a few seconds before deciding that the safest place to be was under Susan's bed. The fight ended when Jeffrey's pillow broke, showering the room with thousands of little white feathers.

Jeffrey sat next to her on her bed, blowing feathers out of his mouth. "What are we going to do now?" he said, grabbing a handful of feathers as they floated down.

"I don't know. That was your pillow." She laughed as she hugged him. Farrun poked his head out, sneezed, and went back under the bed.

Nancy woke them in the morning with a gentle tapping on the door. "Lord Falcon's back. He arrived during the night and left word he'll see you at breakfast."

When Susan and Jeffrey went downstairs, the house was a hive of activity. Everywhere, people were rushing around. Some were carrying furniture out of the house; others were wrapping small things and putting them in wooden boxes. Susan hurried to the dining room and saw Falcon at the table eating. Two places were set next to him.

"Susan, Jeffrey," he said. "You'd better sit and eat. We don't have much time; the king's army is about a day's ride from here. As soon as everything we can carry is packed into wagons, we're leaving."

"Can't you do anything?" asked Susan as she sat down.

"There are too many soldiers and I didn't have time to raise enough men to fight them. Ometerer has moved quicker than I expected."

"I don't understand," said Susan. "You keep talking about Ometerer. Isn't he just the head shaman? A'aster's still the king, isn't he?"

"A'aster's the king, but Ometerer rules. A'aster was never a great king, but he was never vicious until Ometerer rose to the head of his order. He's got A'aster under some sort of spell, and whatever Ometerer wants, A'aster agrees to it."

"What kind of spell?" asked Jeffrey.

"I wish I knew." Falcon shook his head as he ate more porridge. When he had finished, he continued. "Ever since the rebellion four hundred years ago, the kings of Reune have never really trusted anyone with green eyes. But they needed the taxes from the Thorals, and there were always enough green-eyed people living throughout the kingdom to prevent the kings from trying to kill us. About eight years ago, Ometerer suddenly began to rise up in the ranks of the shamans. He's the one behind the new law; he's the one that wants us dead."

"But why?" asked Susan.

"He suspects our power and wants it for himself."

"But that's impossible. If you can't shape-change naturally, no one can teach you."

"We know it, but he doesn't. It took me a few years to find out because I had to get a spy without green eyes into the Order of Shamans. The spy found out that many years ago, while Ometerer was still a novice, he went with several shamans to Yunii."

"That's on the other side of the Thundrous Mountains," Susan said to Jeffrey between bites.

"When Ometerer returned to Reune, he brought back a scroll he had stolen. I saw Ometerer looking at it once, about seven years ago, when I was spying on the king as a rentia . . ."

"Then you *are* a Shape-Changer," said Susan.

"I wouldn't have asked if you were clan if I weren't," he

answered. "But as I was saying, I spied on A'aster because he was beginning to raise taxes, making it harder for the people to survive. If I had known how dangerous the scroll was, I would have destroyed it then."

"Why?" asked Susan. "How can a scroll be dangerous? It's just words."

"Do you remember the spell the wolf broke? The shamans cast their spells by saying words, words that Ometerer got from the scroll. I didn't recognize the language it was written in. Even Ometerer doesn't understand it. But my spy said when Ometerer pronounces some of the words written on the scroll, things happen. Ometerer returned from Yunii six years before he began his rise in the order so it's taken him a long time to figure out the few spells the shamans know."

"You mean like the spell that held us," said Jeffrey.

"Yes. My spy also found out that not everyone who says the words can make the magic work. He couldn't make the words do anything and that's why he'll never be a full shaman."

"But if Ometerer has his own magic, why does he want to kill us?" asked Susan.

"Because," answered Falcon, "the shamans' magic is erratic."

"What?" said Jeffrey.

"It means it doesn't always work. A shaman can say the words one day and cast a spell. But the next day, nothing may happen. Even Ometerer can't make the magic obey him all the time. As I told you, no one knows what language the scroll is written in so it's possible the shamans are doing something wrong. It's also possible they aren't doing enough right, and not knowing is driving Ometerer crazy. Twenty shamans could freeze an army of a thousand men or they could just shout nonsense words and be killed."

"But why . . ." started Susan.

"Does Ometerer want to know our secret? He thinks if he learns the power, he will be able to perform his magic successfully all the time."

"What can we do about it?" asked Susan.

"We have to kill Ometerer and destroy the scroll. He guards it so jealously that he always has it with him and refuses to let even his most trusted people copy it. He's afraid that another shaman might discover more spells before he does. I'm sure that any spell he uses on the king is his secret alone, so if we kill him and destroy the scroll, we will prevent anyone else from controlling the king."

"But the shamans will still be able to do the spells they know," said Susan.

"When I was your age, I played a gossip game. Did you ever play anything like that?"

Susan nodded.

"What's that?" asked Jeffrey.

"I told something to a friend, who told it to someone else, who told it to someone else. By the time the eighth person heard it, it wasn't what I said anymore. The same thing will happen with the shamans' magic. Since there are no copies of the scroll, the words they say will eventually change, and their magic power will die."

"Wh–why do–don't yo–you,"

111

"Easy, Jeffrey," said Falcon, smoothing the boy's hair. "There's nothing for you to get excited about. Just take a breath and start over."

"Why don't you be–become something and kill him?"

"Because I don't know where he is. He never stays in one place more than several weeks."

"But I know where he is," said Susan. "At least I know where he was."

Lord Falcon looked at her. "Before you tell me, tell me about you and Jeffrey."

For the next fifteen minutes, Susan told Lord Falcon everything she could remember from the time she left the Thoral Mountains. When she finished, he just shook his head.

"I never heard of anything like that cave you mentioned. But I agree with you that Jeffrey should be there when we try to figure out how to open the sealed door. What do you say, Jeffrey?"

Jeffrey looked at him and nodded.

"Good," said Falcon. "Now, I will give you two choices and you'll have to decide what to do: First, you can return to the Thoral Mountains. The people have to prepare for an attack, if they haven't already started. Ometerer will not be satisfied until he either learns the secret of the power or kills everyone with the Elders' mark trying to learn it."

"And my other choice?" she asked.

"Return to the castle near the Endless Sea. If Ometerer is there, shape-change and kill him. If you can't kill him, at least destroy the scroll. That would mean that eventually this strange magic will vanish from Reune."

"What about m–me?" asked Jeffrey.

"You'll stay with Susan. You two don't have to decide now what you want to do, but you have to leave. You're not going back the way you came, either. You're going east, into the Thundrous Mountains. Just go a little way up and turn south. If you decide to head for the Thorals, stay in the mountains at least a month before you start turning west. That should put you close to the Thorals. If you decide to go back to the sea, spend about a week traveling south. Become your rentia and look for God's Hand. You have to find the place where you left it so you can safely return to the valley near Lief."

"Why do you want us to go that way?" she asked.

"Because the king's army is closing in on this place. I have planned an escape route for me and my people."

"What are you going to do?"

Lord Falcon, who had finished his breakfast, pushed the plate away from him. Susan saw how tired he looked. "I'm going to take a bath, change my clothes, and burn my house down." Susan and Jeffrey just stared at him. "The army will be here by tomorrow. I don't want to give those . . . people my home."

"But the house?" whispered Susan.

"It's only a house," said Falcon, putting his hand on her shoulder. "Houses can be rebuilt, but lives can't. Some things are not worth dying for, others are. No, children, my house burns. The house burns."

Chapter 10

When Susan and Jeffrey stopped for lunch, smoke filled the sky far behind them. Even Farrun noticed the dark columns. "He must have burned everything," said Susan. "The house, the barns, everything."

"Will he build it again?"

"I hope so. Are you ready? Lord Falcon said we should reach the base of the mountains sometime tomorrow. He said we'll be safe there."

Mounting the horses Falcon had given them, they continued, with the Thundrous Mountains looming larger each time they looked up. When they next stopped, it was late evening. After everyone had eaten, and before curling up into the blankets that were also a present from Lord Falcon, Susan and Jeffrey huddled closer to the flames to keep the chill night air away.

"What are you going to do?" asked Jeffrey.

"I don't know. What do you think?" The boy just shook his head. "What about you, Farrun? Should we go home?"

Farrun didn't answer, either. He licked her cheek several times, then laid his head in her lap and stretched his body over Jeffrey's. Jeffrey didn't mind.

"When are you going to decide?" he asked. Susan just shrugged her shoulders and put more branches on the fire.

Falcon was right, and by late morning of the next day, the land seemed to rise sharply. Farrun ran ahead, appearing at the top of a rock only to jump down and pop up someplace else. "He's happy to be back in real mountains," said Susan. "We'll spend an hour or so riding up and then make our way south. I don't want to give up the horses, and if we go too high we might have to.

"Farrun," she called. "Stop playing! We've got to go. Scout for us. Find the easiest way for the horses." Almost immediately he appeared and began to lead the way. Much later, they stopped.

"I don't like this," she said as they started their fire.

"What?"

"Farrun's taking us more east than south."

"Why are you doing that?" Jeffrey asked him as he kneeled down to pet the wolf. Farrun answered by licking the boy's face then nipping his ear. "Why did he do that?"

"Because he knows better than we do. If he's taking us farther into the mountains, it means that the horses would have a harder time if we stayed lower. I just don't like it."

"Why don't you become a rentia and look for yourself?"

"Because," she said, petting Farrun, "he's the *real* wolf and was born in mountains just like these. You know what you're doing, don't you, Farrun?"

Farrun sneezed, then licked her face without nipping.

115

Days later, Farrun led them down a steep slope. When they reached the bottom, Susan saw they were in a narrow valley that stretched for miles in front of them. "The valley heads southeast," she said. "When we get to the end of it, we turn west, back to Reune."

"Have you decided? Are we going to Nieswim's castle?"

"I don't know," she answered. "I really don't. The farther east we move, the closer we get to either Yunii or Kestra, the two countries nearest to us. We can decide where to go when we see our border. What do you want to do?"

"I haven't thought about it. As long as the three of us stay together, it doesn't matter."

"Don't worry about that, Clan-brother. We'll be together a long time. Promise."

They moved quickly now, the horses trotting easily on the valley floor. Several times Farrun made them wait while he scouted ahead, but nothing frightened him. Susan camped early that night and told Farrun to go hunting, for both himself and them. She was tired of eating dried meat and journey cakes. It took over an hour for the wolf to return with dinner.

The twin moons were in the middle of the sky when drops of rain woke Susan. At first, she just pulled the blanket over herself and tried to sleep. But the rain got heavier. She got up and threw the rest of the branches on the dying coals, but the fire just hissed and sputtered. She began to shiver as water soaked through the blanket. By this time, Jeffrey was up, too.

"Saddle the horses," she said. "We'll ride for the valley edge. Maybe we can find some rocks to hide under."

A streak of lightning slammed into the ground, and almost immediately afterward a loud clap of thunder cracked in the sky. Rain poured down as if the bottom of the giant cloud above had vanished, dropping all the water inside at once. As Susan tried to hold the reins of her frightened horse with one hand and throw the saddle over its back with the other, she noticed that she was standing in a stream of water. When a second bolt of lightning lit the sky, she looked up. Water was pouring down into the valley from all sides.

Farrun pushed his head into her legs and growled.

"Jeffrey," she shouted over the thunder ringing in her ears. "Jeffrey!" She let her horse go and ran to him. By now, the noise of the rain was so loud Susan had to yell in his ear. "Let the horse go! Hurry! Change into your panther. Follow me."

"Wh–what?" he mouthed.

"Change into your panther!" Susan closed her eyes and concentrated. She used the power — but Jeffrey didn't. The Susan-wolf saw the twelve-year-old as he was, a wet, frightened, little boy. She saw him squeeze his eyes shut, but she didn't see him change. She became herself again.

"You must try. Jeffrey, please try harder. We have to get out of here now!"

"I ca–can't. I'm . . ."

Farrun howled.

Susan pulled Jeffrey into her and hugged him tightly. As the thunder boomed again, she spoke directly into his ear. "The panther is your second form, Clan-brother. It is part of you. You can do it. You can." She kissed the top of his head and backed up. Holding on to his hand, she called. "Use the power, Jeffrey. Become your panther!"

This time, instead of closing his eyes, Jeffrey looked at her. As soon as he began his transformation, she let go and became her wolf.

Three animals raced to the edge of the valley, trying to find a place to climb. But whenever the Susan-wolf jumped, the sheets of water pouring off the rocks and grass slopes kept throwing her back. And each time she fell, the water on the valley floor was slightly higher. The Susan-wolf looked at Farrun and howled, telling him he had to find another way out; the valley floor was beginning to fill up!

Again and again, lightning flared in the sky and again and again claps of thunder covered the howling of the wolves and the hissing of an angry panther. The Susan-wolf turned when Farrun nipped her; she saw him bite the Jeffrey-panther, too, then back off quickly when the Jeffrey-panther struck out at him with sharp, feline claws. Farrun ran farther down the valley and the Susan-wolf, after waiting for the Jeffrey-panther to follow, ran after them.

The valley sloped downward as it neared its narrow end, and the pooling water was already so deep that Farrun had to jump into a small but growing lake. He began swimming. The Susan-wolf waited again until the Jeffrey-panther was in the water before jumping in. She swam her fastest, moving four legs in a dog-paddle. She saw Farrun reach the end of the valley and jump out on a rock ledge. She swam alongside the Jeffrey-panther and nudged him toward Farrun. But a panther-Jeffrey snarled and lashed out with his teeth, biting her on the back of her neck.

Susan felt the pain and her concentration faltered. She found herself, all Susan, floundering in the rising water as her woolen dress pulled her down. "Farrun!" She tried to swim but was too tired. Her head went under. Something slammed into her body. Her arms instinctively wrapped around it, hoping it would keep her afloat. Wet fur pressed against her cheek and she knew Farrun was there. Slowly, the large wolf swam with her until they reached the rock ledge that a soaked, hissing panther-Jeffrey now possessed. Susan let go. When Farrun jumped up, the panther-Jeffrey attacked and forced him back into the water.

Susan was exhausted. She tried to lift herself up but had strength only to cling to the ledge. "Jeffrey . . . Jeffrey, remember who you are! Remember!"

The hissing panther-Jeffrey jumped at her and swung his paws at her hands.

"Jeffrey!" Susan shouted in the cat's ear as she slid back into the water. Again, Farrun was there, helping her to reach the surface. But he was breathing hard.

As she slipped under the water once again, hands gripped her upraised arms. "Su–Susan! I–I'm sor–" He didn't finish as he pulled. Susan reached the ledge, and with Jeffrey's help managed to get up. Then she leaned down, and using what strength she had left, pulled Farrun up.

But Farrun wasn't satisfied when he stood on the ledge. The rain plunged down in continuous sheets of water.

Lightning constantly lit the sky. Thunder echoed off the valley walls. Farrun snapped his jaws at Susan's feet, pushing her and Jeffrey farther along the ledge. The ledge ended and Jeffrey saw water spilling out of the valley beneath them, cutting off their escape. But starting at the end of the ledge, and growing up the sides of the mountain, were tall, sturdy trees. Jeffrey let Susan squeeze by him. Reaching up, she wrapped one arm around the closest tree trunk and held on to it while helping Jeffrey join her. When they were several feet up the mountain, Farrun jumped.

Moving from trunk to trunk, pounded by the deafening sound of the mighty thunder and pouring rain, the three climbed higher up the steep mountain slope. After what seemed hours, Susan saw a small flat spot of ground completely surrounded by trees. She worked her way there, holding on to one tree trunk with one arm until her hand was almost touching another. She reached the clearing and fell down, exhausted.

When she woke, the sky was clear, the sun was just rising, and Farrun was sleeping next to her, nose tucked under her chin. She reached out and hugged him tightly, feeling slow and gentle licks on her cheek. But when his tongue touched the back of her neck, she felt a sharp pain. Then she remembered. "Where's Jeffrey?" Her body ached, her muscles were sore, and Jeffrey was gone.

"He has to be somewhere near here," she said, slowly getting up. "Let's find him." It wasn't hard. Though there were no tracks or scent for Farrun to follow, the only direction the boy could have gone was up. In less than five minutes, she saw him curled up in a ball, sleeping under a pine tree. Susan crawled under the branch and woke him up.

Jeffrey's eyes slowly opened. When he realized Susan was next to him, he quickly scurried out and tried to run away. Farrun stopped him.

"What's the matter with you?" asked Susan.

"Wh–wh–what's the ma–ma–matter? I–I al–almost ki–killed you! I al–almost killed him, too," he said, looking at Farrun. "Lo–look wh–what I di–did to you." He pointed to the cut on her neck. "Le–le–leave me here. I . . . I . . ."

"You stop that!" said Susan, raising her voice sharply. Then, as she stood up, she took a breath. "I'm sorry I yelled. Come here. Please." When Jeffrey didn't, she went to him. She took his hand and sat on the soggy ground, pulling him down. "Last night, when you were almost dying, you forgot who you were and let the panther control you. Ever since Rillan discovered I had the power, I have been taught how to use it. I've been doing this for years, but when you bit me, I forgot to concentrate and almost killed myself and Farrun, too. You didn't make me break my concentration, I did it myself. It was my fault, Jeffrey, my fault."

"Bu–but I hurt you."

"Shape-Changers sometimes have to fight as animals, and if they can't get hurt while being their animals, then maybe . . . then maybe they don't deserve to call themselves Shape-Changers. You did more last night than anyone could have asked of you. I didn't. How many times have you been your panther? Ten? Twenty? And each time, the only thing we did was play. You may not believe this, but I'm proud of you because you became your panther when you had to. You ran and jumped and swam as your animal. And only in the end, when you were exhausted, did you forget."

"B–but I . . ."

"Listen to me, Jeffrey. It's true the panther controlled you for a while. But in the end, when you had to remember who you were, you did. You changed back and pulled me out of the water. You didn't almost kill me. You saved me. Rillan will not be proud of what I did last night. But he'll say you did your best, your very best."

Farrun came and sat between them. He licked her cheek and then Jeffrey's.

"See," said Susan. "He's not angry; he understands."

"B–but I d–did tha–that?" he said raising a hand to point to her neck again.

"You didn't do it. The animal's instinct did."

"You–you're not angry?"

"Not at you. If I have to be angry with anyone, it's with me. I guess I still have a lot to learn about being a Shape-Changer."

Jeffrey gave her a big hug, one that Susan returned just as hard. "Wh–what are we going to do now? We lost everything Lord Falcon gave us when the horses ran away. Maybe we should go back to Reune. I've never been in a storm that bad before."

Susan thought for a moment. "You're right. I forgot why these are called the Thundrous Mountains. Storms like the one we had last night are common during the summer.

We'll leave the mountains quickly and head west. We're going home."

Just at that moment, Farrun tilted his head as if he was listening to something. He yelped once, ran a few yards farther up the mountain, stopped and yelped again. When he saw Susan and Jeffrey looking at him, he continued running uphill.

"What . . ."

"I don't know," answered Susan. "Come on, we have to follow him."

Farrun waited for them, then turned and ran along the top of the hill. Tucked in between two large boulders was a small path, and as soon as Susan saw where he was going, Farrun squeezed between the rocks and disappeared. They followed the path up for a while until Susan stopped short.

Farrun was sitting, wagging his tail in front of a large cat. Susan guessed it weighed close to fifteen pounds. But it wasn't fat; it was well built and muscular. Its paws and chest were white. Streaks of white moved up the cat's sides until they gradually changed to orange. Its back was orange with black lines running across it, and its slowly switching orange tail had black bands circling it.

"That's strange," said Susan.

"The cat?"

"No, Farrun. He doesn't like cats. He still chases them all the time. I wonder why he's being friendly with that one?" When Susan saw Farrun lean forward and lick the cat once on its nose, she shook her head. Suddenly, the cat ran off and Farrun followed.

"Come on," said Susan. "Something's not right." She followed her wolf for a short distance to a lean-to crumpled oddly against the side of a huge boulder. The rain the night before must have loosened the soil and the boulder had shifted. She saw a man, facing away from her, straining to push the huge rock, and when Susan took a step closer, she saw why. Someone else was pinned beneath it.

Without hesitating, Susan ran to the rock and put her shoulder next to the man's. When he turned his head and noticed her, Susan looked closer at him. He could have been her age, or just a little older. He stared at her with black eyes and a face streaked with dirt.

"We'll try together," she said. The youth silently nodded. "One, two, three!" She pushed with whatever strength she had but it was no use. The rock wouldn't budge. Susan looked around the young man to see a girl lying on the ground, face up, her arm pinned under the boulder. The girl, too, was Susan's age. Her eyes were half open, and the pain on her face was easy to read.

"Let's try again," she said. "Jeffrey, help us." The three of them pushed. Nothing happened.

Farrun poked his head into Susan and growled. The orange-and-black cat sat next to him looking up.

I could save her! But Rillan said never change in front of anyone. I did it once and I promised Farrun I'd learn from it. How can I save her and keep the secret at the same time?

The cat meowed loudly and Farrun pushed Susan a second time. "Rillan said I shouldn't," she snapped at Farrun. "He said 'never, never, never!'"

For the first time since Farrun was a half-grown cub who didn't know better, he snapped at Susan, biting her leg just enough to break the skin under the dress. Farrun didn't want the girl to die.

"Move away from the rock," said Susan to the young man. He ignored her and put his shoulder back to try again. "I said get away!" she shouted, pushing him. "I'll do it. You just pull her out when the rock rolls off."

I have to. Susan stood next to the rock and concentrated. This time, instead of shrinking, her body grew. Her wet dress melted into her skin and became chocolate brown. Her arms grew longer and reached the ground, turning large, heavy, and thick to match her two hind legs. Her head grew and thickened, her nose widened. Two horns sprouted from her skull above her eyes and spread out, covering a span of at least four feet.

A wild terano, a bull-like animal known throughout Reune for its strength and power, stood and looked down at a girl pinned beneath the rock.

Move the rock, but don't step on the girl.
MOVE.

The Susan-terano walked to the side of the rock and placed her legs carefully over the girl. When she lowered her head, her horns reached the two edges of the boulder. The animal pushed but the rock didn't move.

HARD-HEA-VY, the terano-mind thought as the Susan-bull backed up a step.

Hurry. We must do it. We must move the rock now!

The Susan-terano pawed the ground with a front leg, almost hitting the trapped girl. She raised her head, stretching her neck as she screamed a long, loud bellow. Then she put her head back to the rock and walked forward. The boulder moved. The Susan-terano felt the young man shove his way between her hind legs in order to reach the girl. When the girl's arm was clear, the huge animal stepped away. The rock rolled back.

Concentrate. Become yourself. Slowly, the large bull shrank and Susan became herself.

The girl looked at Susan, her eyes and mouth open. Her head moved and she fell unconscious.

I had to do it.

Chapter 11

Susan stepped toward the young man, who was now carefully cutting away the girl's shirtsleeve. As she stepped closer, the cat hissed. Farrun moved in front of Susan and pushed gently with his head.

"Farrun!"

The cat hissed again. Farrun, putting his paws on her shoulders and licking her cheek, pushed her back several more steps.

"What's wrong with him?" asked Jeffrey.

"I don't think the cat wants me to help, and I think Farrun agrees. All right, Farrun. We'll leave them alone."

"How would Farrun know?" asked Jeffrey. Susan just shrugged her shoulders. "What are you going to tell them when they ask about you?"

Susan didn't answer right away. *What AM I going to say?* She put her arm around Jeffrey and leaned her head on his. "I don't know, Clan-brother."

"You had to do it. If you hadn't, she would have died."

"But I was told not to. Rillan told me so many times I got tired of hearing it. Never use the power in front of anyone who isn't clan or family. Never."

"But Rillan wasn't here," he answered. "He wouldn't have let her die, would he? How can he tell you what you can never do when he's not here?"

Farrun came and lifted the bottom of her dress with his nose. He licked the place where he had bitten her, then moved around Jeffrey and pushed him slightly, knocking him into Susan.

"Why did you do that?" Jeffrey asked. "I didn't say anything wrong."

"No," said Susan, hugging him. "You said something right. For years I've had things drilled into me, things I should do, things I shouldn't do. Maybe some of the shouldn'ts can be shoulds sometimes. Maybe the nevers I've been taught should not always be nevers. The boy I saved as a fish is alive . . . that girl is alive. Maybe instead of relying only on what I've been taught, I should rely more on myself. It's time for me to make my own decisions, and use the power the way I think it should be used. What do you think, Farrun?"

The wolf rubbed his head against her leg, and when she lowered her hand to scratch him, he gently took it in his mouth.

The three of them sat and watched the young man remove pieces of cloth that had stuck to the girl's arm. "Can't you do anything?" said Jeffrey.

Susan shook her head. "I'm not a healer." She saw that parts of the girl's fingers were crushed, but most of the arm was just red and blood ran from open cuts all along it. "She's lucky," Susan whispered. "The soil was so soggy that the rock pushed her arm down instead of crushing it. Her hand must have been under something hard, though. I hope he knows what he's doing. If he doesn't stop the bleeding soon, she'll die."

The trio looked on as the youth sat even with the girl's chest and rested her bruised arm over his lap. The large cat moved opposite him. Then the young man closed his eyes and remained still. After several minutes, Jeffrey leaned toward Susan and whispered.

"Wh–what's he doing?"

Susan didn't answer. All she could do was point. Blood that had been freely soaking into the ground began to slow and stop. Open cuts and gashes along the girl's entire arm began to close. Skin that had been ripped and draped loosely over the arm moved by itself, going back to the places it had come from. The youth remained, not moving, for more than twenty minutes. But when he finally took a deep breath and opened his eyes, the girl's arm looked almost normal, except that the skin was blotched with red.

When Susan began to rise, the cat looked at her. Farrun put his head in her lap and began to lick her arm. Neither animal wanted Susan to get up.

The young man took another deep breath and gently placed the girl's damaged hand on the ground. Susan saw it clearly now; the palm and last three fingers were crushed. The cat walked around the unconscious girl and sat next to the youth. It placed its paws on his knee and began kneading, spreading its claws slightly and pushing against the knee one paw at a time. The youth closed his eyes; the cat sat motionless.

Susan and Jeffrey waited . . . and waited. The sun moved higher and still neither youth nor cat stirred. It could have been another twenty minutes or it could have been an hour. Susan didn't know. Then she saw the impossible.

The crushed hand quivered. The flattened fingers thickened; the flattened palm thickened. Her hand healed! The cat meowed. The young man opened his eyes, leaned back, and fell.

Susan quickly rose. The cat didn't object and neither did Farrun as she ran to the lying figures. "Farrun, find something to eat. Jeffrey, those must be their travel-packs." She pointed toward the part of the lean-to that was still standing. "See if there's anything clean enough for me to use as a bandage. Then try to find enough dry wood for a fire."

While Jeffrey was busy doing what Susan had asked, she carefully moved the girl onto a patch of sunny, almost dry, ground. Next, Susan dragged the youth into the sunlight. Jeffrey came and handed her a clean shirt. Susan wrapped it carefully around the girl's reddened arm and hand. Then she helped Jeffrey start a fire.

When Farrun came back, he was dragging a small deer. Susan had reached down for her knife before she realized it was missing. Everything they had owned had been washed away the night before. But the young man did have a knife, and the blade was sharp.

"Look," said Jeffrey, who was trying to fix the lean-to, "there's a small pot here."

"Farrun," said Susan, "take Jeffrey and find a stream. "Fill the pot with water. I'll make soup even though we have nothing to put in but meat."

When Jeffrey returned, the fire was going, and Susan had finished cutting up the deer. The cat was off to one side eating, and Susan gave Farrun a large part of the deer and told him to do the same. Then, she put the pot next to the flames and waited for the water to boil. Strips of meat roasted on sticks over the fire, and when they were cooked, she and Jeffrey ate.

"What did he do?" Jeffrey asked. "How could he fix her hand like that?"

"I don't know," answered Susan. "I've never seen anything like it. It was magic, Jeffrey. Real magic!"

"Shaman magic?"

"The shamans' magic is evil. This wasn't."

About an hour later, Susan heard the young man move. She ran to him and kneeled by his head. His eyes opened and immediately he sat up. His first thought was for the girl. He slowly unwrapped the shirt that Susan had put on. He looked at Susan, pointed to the sun and then to the girl's arm. Instead of putting the shirt back, he folded it and put it under her head. Then he stood.

"My name's Susan," she said. "That's Jeffrey by the fire, and Farrun's over there."

The youth looked at her. His brow wrinkled as he stared. He turned and pointed to the rock Susan had moved. Then he lightly touched her on her shoulders and lifted his arms high and spread them out. He looked back toward the rock, made a pushing motion with his hands, and placed an open palm on her chest.

"If you're asking me if I became an animal to move the rock, the answer is yes."

131

The young man stepped back and nodded his head. He stared at her for a long time. Susan had the oddest feeling that as his dark eyes looked at her, he was seeing deep into her and stealing all the secrets she wanted to keep to herself. Then he smiled, walked to the fire, and began to eat.

Susan came and sat next to him. "I know you can understand me," she said, "but can't you talk?"

The youth looked at her but the only answer she got was his taking another strip of meat.

The cat meowed and walked to the sleeping girl. Susan, Jeffrey, and the young man went to her, too. Her eyes were open.

"Hello," said Susan.

The girl looked up, blinking as she stared into the sun. Then her eyes focused on Susan. The girl sucked in a quick breath; her eyes opened wide — her face tightened. She was afraid. Without getting up, she kicked out with her feet and scrambled backward. But the youth grabbed her under her shoulders and pulled her into a sitting position. "What . . . what are you?" stammered the girl. She looked beyond Susan to the rock that had pinned her. "How did you do that?"

Susan didn't know what to say so she said nothing.

"Who are you?" asked the girl again.

"I'm someone who helped you," said Susan.

"How?" asked the girl. "How did you do it? No one can do what you did! Not even a sorceress, and the last sorceress died a thousand years ago. What magic do you know? What kind of magic is it?" When Susan didn't answer, the girl spoke again. "I have to know. What kind of magic did you do?"

"I'm not a sorceress," said Susan, "I'm just someone who was here when you needed help."

"People don't change into animals! They can't." When she tried to stand up, the young man helped her. That's when she noticed her arm. She remained very quiet as she studied it and her hand. "Sorceresses do this."

"I didn't do that," said Susan.

"How can you say that? My hand was crushed, I felt it. Not even a Magician of the First Order could heal it. What kind of magic did you use? Was it dark magic?"

"I don't know how to do magic," answered Susan.

"What do you call . . . that?" said the girl, pointing to the boulder. "Of course it's magic. What do you call this?" she added, raising her healed hand. "I asked you what kind of magic you used. Why won't you tell me? Was it dark magic?"

"I told you, I didn't fix your hand."

"He did," said Jeffrey, looking at the silent young man.

"No," said the girl. "He couldn't have. He can't speak. That's impossible."

"He d–did. And the cat helped, too."

"The sirnee?" Susan saw the girl stare at the cat sunning itself on a nearby rock. "He's just a cat."

"But they did it," said Jeffrey again.

"Is that true?" The girl turned around to face the youth, who just looked backed at her. Her voice rose. "Tristan, is it true!"

Susan was so startled she stepped back.

"I asked you if you did this!" the girl yelled again, holding up her arm. This time, he nodded. The girl rubbed her other hand against her cheek and Susan heard her taking deep breaths. "How could you do that! How can you use the magic without saying the words? You didn't just start a fire, you used magic — powerful magic. You have to say the words and you can't speak!"

Susan felt embarrassed; she didn't know what to do. *Why is she so angry? He saved her life, and instead of thanking him, she's screaming. I don't understand.*

"Why are you letting me stay with you?" the girl continued. Susan saw the girl's eyes redden as she paused for a breath. "You don't need me. I'll never be a magician. I can't do anything right. I couldn't make the spell to keep us safe work, and I said the words right. I did! All I am is a tagalong. I'm going to get you killed if I stay with you. Do you understand that!" Her voice cracked and she half cried her next sentence. "I want to go back to Deventap. Go on without me, Tristan. I can't help you." She sat down and stared at the ground.

Tristan shook his head as he looked at her. Then he went to the fire and picked up a freshly cooked piece of meat. He walked back, kneeled, and handed it to the girl.

Susan saw the girl take a deep breath, close her eyes, and silently move her lips. When she opened her eyes, she seemed more relaxed. Holding the meat between her teeth as she pulled the stick out, the girl chewed it slowly and swallowed before continuing.

"I'm . . . I'm sorry," she said to Tristan. "You saved my life and I yelled at you. I shouldn't have done that." He looked at her once and walked back to the fire.

Now the girl turned and looked up at Susan and Jeffrey. She closed her eyes briefly and took another deep breath.

"I don't know who you are . . . I don't know what you are, but you saved my life, too. Thank you."

"My name's Susan, this is Jeffrey, and that's Farrun. If you'd like to thank me, then promise never to tell anyone what happened, what you saw, what I did."

"Wha–what's a Magician of the First Order?" asked Jeffrey.

"You're not from Kestra, are you?" said the girl.

"No," answered Susan. "We come from Reune."

"My name's Maria. This is Tristan. I call the sirnee Jerold." Maria rose, went to the fire, and sat. She was quiet for several minutes as she sipped the soup Tristan had pointed to. "What are you?" Maria finally asked Susan. "What magic do you use? I've never heard of anyone doing what you did."

"And I never heard of anyone doing what he did," said Susan, looking at Tristan.

No one said anything, and the only thing Susan heard was the chewing sounds Tristan made as he ate. *How can I tell her? What would Rillan say if he found out I told someone from another country about the power? Maybe some of the things Rillan taught me will have to be changed. But not this. I can't do it. I just can't!* The silence dragged on until Tristan broke the stick his meat was on. He looked at Susan and then to Maria. He touched his ear and put a finger to his closed lips.

"I think he means that we each have our secrets," said Maria.

There was silence as Susan reached out and took another meat strip. *I should ask her about her magic. Maybe she knows about the shamans' magic and can tell me something to help fight it. But if she tells me, I'll have to tell her about the Elders' power. I can't say anything about that.*

"It's all right," Maria finally said. "You don't have to say anything if you don't want to. I may not be a very good magician, but I know that magicians guard their magic. I won't ask you again. You did enough."

Susan smiled, and the two girls spent a brief moment looking into each other's eyes.

"What did Tristan do?" asked Jeffrey. "Can anyone learn to do it? Could I?"

"I don't know what he did. I really don't. You see, Tristan . . ." Maria stopped in the middle of her sentence. She watched the wood burn as she slowly finished her soup. "I can't tell you, Jeffrey. I'm sorry, but I can't."

When everyone finished eating, Susan stood up. "We have to leave," she said. "Our clan is in danger, and we're going home to help."

Maria nodded her head. "Things aren't going well in Kestra, either. That's why we're here. The king of Yunii wants to rule the four nations and has attacked us. We're going to Yunii and try to steal some of their magic."

"I hope you find what you're looking for," said Susan.

Maria reached out her hand and touched Susan's. "I don't understand who you are or what you can do. But I promise we'll never tell anyone what happened. I just wish there was something more I could do to repay you."

"Keeping my secret is enough."

Maria shook her head. "Jeffrey, I can't tell you what you wanted to know. But there's someone else who might. Her name is Befany. She lives in Deventap and when we get home, we'll be staying with her. I can't promise, but if everything works out for you and your clan, come to see us. I'll ask Befany to tell you."

"Befany. I'll remember her name. Thank you, Maria. Come on, Farrun," Susan said. "Let's go." Without looking back, the three of them walked away from the fire.

Chapter 12

Farrun led the way down the slope, which was still slippery from the last night's rain. Susan stumbled and skidded on her rear several feet, stopping only when she grabbed a tree.

"Why don't we become our animals?" said Jeffrey, sliding to a stop next to her. "No one's around. Do you think Farrun can lead us out of here by tonight?"

Susan remained on the ground for a minute catching her breath. Farrun sat a few feet in front of her. "What do you think, Farrun? Can we be out of these mountains by tonight?"

Farrun tilted his head.

"I don't know if that means yes or no," said Susan, rubbing both sides of his head. "Let's see how good you really are at finding your way."

One wolf, one Susan-wolf, and one Jeffrey-panther ran, walked, and trotted the rest of the day and well into the night. They stopped only to drink, and just as the moons were overhead, the land finally began to flatten out. A tired Jeffrey and Susan became themselves.

The first thing they did was start a fire while Farrun disappeared into the night. When he returned, with a bird, the fire was hot. Though Susan and Jeffrey were half asleep as she prepared the bird, they were too hungry to wait until morning to eat. The bird was small, and while Farrun ran off again to hunt his own dinner, they ate. When the two of them went to sleep, though they weren't full, they weren't hungry.

In the morning, Susan and Jeffrey walked the rest of the way as themselves, stopping just inside the last clump of trees.

"It's not going to be easy now," Susan said. "Somewhere west of us is God's Hand, I think. I'll fly there first to make sure. We won't find anything to eat or drink on the way so we're going to be thirsty. The next time we take a drink will be when we get to the tub room, if we find the entrance."

"We'll be all right," said Jeffrey. "Things haven't been easy for us since we met. They can't get much harder."

Susan leaned over and kissed him. "We'll start a fire before I leave, and Farrun will catch something for you to eat. Do the best you can cooking it; I'll eat when I come back. Watch my clan-brother, Farrun, and yes, even before you ask, I'll be careful."

Warning Jeffrey to stay in the trees until she returned, she walked to the beginning of the desertlike land and concentrated.

This time, as the Susan-bird hopped on the ground, pecking in the dirt for insects, Susan's mind did not have to argue with the rentia's mind. There was nothing to frighten the little bird.

Fly, and the Susan-bird took off. As the Susan-rentia watched the land beneath her, it looked the same as when she had left the Elders' cave, low bushes and dry earth. Every so often, she saw hoof prints in the sandy soil. Though she didn't see anyone, the land was obviously not as empty as she had thought. After half an hour and several other sets of tracks, Susan realized that she would have to come up with a better idea. She couldn't risk two wolves and a panther being seen crossing this land; and without water, she and Jeffrey couldn't make it in their true forms. She landed on a bush and looked at the mountains in front of her. God's Hand was still far away. It would take several days of walking, and even though summer was passing quickly, it would be a long, hot, dry walk.

Fly. Fly northward. An hour later, a nearly exhausted Susan-rentia finally found a stream. Before landing, she soared up just to make sure the land was completely deserted. Then Susan became herself and took a deep, long drink. She sat on the shady side of a large bush to rest and think. This was the beginning of the end of the desert and the naked rock peaks of God's Hand Mountains were all she could see. But she was so far from the Thundrous Mountains that even their shadow had disappeared from the horizon.

Should I teach Jeffrey to become a rentia? Then we could do it. But as soon as the thought left her mind, the answer entered it. *No, it's too dangerous. Maybe I could become a horse and have him ride me?* But a horse also needs water, and if they did see anyone, she couldn't change back. There was only one answer, one she didn't like. She would have to fly to a village, change into herself, and steal a water pouch and a small sack for carrying food. Then she would have to become a bird large enough to carry the supplies, an eagle or a hawk. She'd have to do everything without being seen, and that wouldn't be easy. There were no forests or clumps of trees to hide her transforming.

When half an hour passed, and Susan felt her strength returning, she took one more drink before becoming her bird again. *Fly,* she thought to the rentia-mind. *Fly back to the mountains.* It was late in the afternoon before she returned. Jeffrey and Farrun were standing at the edge of the treeline looking into the desert. The wolf saw the small Susan-rentia and began wagging his tail even before she landed. When she was all Susan, Farrun jumped on her, licking, wagging his whole rear, sniffing, and licking again.

The first thing she did was follow Jeffrey to a stream and drink. Then she ate and told him and Farrun what she had seen and planned to do.

Farrun growled, wrapping his teeth around her wrist. Even Jeffrey knew what that meant. "He doesn't want you to do it, and I think he's right. It's too dangerous."

"Without food and water, we'll never make it. If I don't steal at least a water pouch, we'll have to stay in the Thundrous Mountains and backtrack almost to Falcon's land. That's even more dangerous."

"We could stay in the mountains and go south. Falcon said we should do that if we decided to go to the Thorals."

"Don't tell me you forgot the storm already. Without supplies or horses, it might take us two months to reach the end of the Thundrous Mountains. No, Jeffrey, we have to go back to God's Hand. When we come out of the Elders' cave, we should be able to steal enough to feed ourselves while we head for Nieswim's castle. Let's just hope Ometerer is still there."

"Then teach me to become a bird."

Susan pulled him close in a tight hug. "Clan-brother, do you remember I told you what Maklin said about things you can do and things you can't?" She didn't wait for him to answer. "That's something I can't. I have become very fond of you and I don't want anything to happen to you."

"But we're going to O–Ometerer. Something could happen to me then."

"It might, but not before Farrun and I do everything we can to try to stop it. If something happened while you were another animal, it would be my fault. I know I've made mistakes, but I won't make this one. Tomorrow I'm going to find a village, wait as my rentia until dark, and steal what I can."

"But how do you know you can't teach me?" said Jeffrey. "You told me I have a lot of power. Teach me how to become a rentia. I can do it, I know I can! Then we can fly to God's Hand together."

Susan looked at him. *Should I try?* After a moment, she decided. "I can't Jeffrey. I just can't."

In the morning, when Susan woke up, Jeffrey was gone. Farrun quickly sniffed the ground and ran to the beginning of the dry land. A set of panther tracks headed straight for God's Hand Mountains.

"Why didn't you hear him get up?" she snapped as she walked back into the trees.

Farrun growled and pushed against her with his head.

"Well, I was tired! I spent most of the day flying back and forth."

142

Farrun growled again as he poked his nose at a cooked rabbit lying near the dead ashes.

"You were tired, too. You hunted most of the day. I'm sorry," she said, petting him and letting him lick her face, "getting upset won't help us. Come on, Farrun, let's go find him." Before leaving, she and Farrun stopped to eat; when they left there would be no way to carry the food.

Within minutes, two wolves were trotting into the desert. Though Farrun led, the Susan-wolf knew where the Jeffrey-panther had gone. The scent was fresh. Farrun set a brisk pace, but when they stopped to rest, the Susan-wolf saw no sign of the black panther. But she saw something else, something that frightened her.

Covering the horizon in front of them was a huge dark cloud. Farrun sniffed the air, then backed up next to Susan, pushing her down and lying on top of her. The Susan-wolf felt it, a hot, dry wind coming at them from the west. As the wind picked up speed, Susan knew what the cloud was — a dust storm!

Farrun pushed against her until she moved her backside toward the wind. When the first spears of dirt hit her, the Susan-wolf tucked her head under Farrun's shoulder and closed her eyes.

The wind howled. Dirt, pebbles, and small rocks, hurtling toward the Thundrous Mountains, rubbed against her fur like sandpaper. The Susan-wolf pushed her nose deeper into Farrun's fur and heard his low growl above the sound of the storm. She growled back telling him she was fine. The Susan-wolf lost track of time. Twice Farrun moved — shifting position while keeping his body low against the ground and shaking himself free of dirt — before sitting on top of Susan again. If he hadn't done that, Susan thought, the two of them might have been buried alive.

But finally the wind died, sand and dirt became too heavy for it and fell; the storm was over. Far behind her, the Susan-wolf heard the low rumble of thunder. As the hot wind raced up the side of the Thundrous Mountains, it quickly cooled, and the sudden drop in air temperature began fueling another of the severe storms the mountains were noted for.

Susan thought of herself and changed to her human form. Then, she waited until Farrun had licked her face clean before speaking. "We'll never trail him now. All we can do is make for God's Hand. If he didn't panic in the storm, if he stayed in his animal form and waited it out as we did, he'll be all right."

Farrun growled softly.

"I know," she said, rubbing her cheek against his, "that's a lot of ifs. But all we can do is hope." She became her wolf and they started for God's Hand.

In the early evening, Farrun stopped. He ran back and forth across the ground, sniffing. The Susan-wolf did the same, and after a moment she knew what he had found. *Horses. There would be no traces of anything passing before the storm. That means these horses were just here!* She sat and looked at Farrun. It was at times like these she wished she could speak to his mind. She wondered if anywhere in the world of Enstor, such a magic existed. If it did, wouldn't it be great if she . . .

Farrun's growl stopped her daydreaming. He had finished smelling and wanted to continue. She, on the other hand, didn't. She poked her nose into the scent and started off in the direction it was strongest.

Farrun blocked her.

We have to see if they found Jeffrey, Susan thought. The Susan-wolf pushed him gently in the direction she wanted to go. Farrun nipped her ear, telling her he didn't think it was a good idea, but he put his nose back to the ground and followed the scent. Being a real wolf, his senses were sharper than hers.

The night was clear as the two wolves moved northwest. The twin moons lit the ground well enough for them to see, and when the faint halo of a campfire glowed in the distance, both wolves saw it. Farrun growled. The Susan-wolf nodded her head; she didn't need to be reminded of what had happened the last time she spied on a campsite.

Farrun moved in a wide circle, approaching the camp from downwind. If he hadn't, the horses would have smelled them and become alarmed.

The Susan-wolf inched up, staying just outside the glow of the fire. It was late and everyone was sleeping. She saw no guards, only ten bodies on the ground, all covered with blankets. She poked her head up and sniffed. The scents carried on the air told her nothing.

But they did tell Farrun something. He had a big advantage over her; he remembered what Jeffrey smelled like. He pushed against her, pointing with his nose. From where she lay, she couldn't see which one was Jeffrey. She backed up; Farrun followed. Sounds carry easily in the night, so without speaking, Susan first became herself and then her rentia.

Fly to the light. Fly near the fire.

NO-SAFE-NO-SEE-WELL-NO-FLY-NIGHT.

Yes, I tell you! Fly to the fire!

NO-FIRE-NO-FIRE-NO-FIRE . . .

Suddenly, a huge dark shape appeared in front of the Susan-rentia.

FLY-FLY-FLY!

The Susan-rentia was in the air. She went toward the light because the bird's instincts would not let her fly into the dark desert. She landed on the rear of one of the horses instead of the ground near the fire. The horse knew the bird was there and swished its tail. But the tail missed and the Susan-rentia stayed. Rentias often landed and ate small insects off the backs of animals that didn't bother or frighten them, so the rentia's mind wasn't afraid of the swinging tail. But that didn't help Susan; she still couldn't see which of the ten sleeping forms was Jeffrey's. She would have to get closer.

Concentrate, she told herself, *concentrate!* The Susan-rentia flew down and hopped along the ground. A rustling blanket startled it.

Don't fly! she thought before the bird could even move its wings. The Susan-rentia hopped toward the movement. It was Jeffrey. He was lying on his back, eyes open, taking soft, quick breaths. Susan saw why. His arms were stretched out and tied tightly to stakes pounded into the ground. Jeffrey could not turn into his panther because his front paws, spread too far apart for a panther, would still

146

be securely tied. But she had to let him know she was there.

Hop on his chest. Let him see we are here.

NO-NO, answered the rentia-mind. *DAN-GER.*

There's no danger. The boy is our friend.

The Susan-rentia flapped its wings and hopped onto Jeffrey's chest. Jeffrey felt the bird and looked as far down as he could without moving his head. He saw her. "I–I–I'm s–s–sor–ry," he whispered. The Susan-rentia flew away.

Chapter 13

Susan and Farrun sat in the dark, half a mile from the men who held Jeffrey captive. Susan was cold, tired, hungry, and thirsty, but there was nothing she could do about anything. So she sat, resting her head against Farrun.

"Jeffrey told me he wanted to learn to be a rentia and I said no. I should have guessed he would try something stupid like running off. He's only twelve. Wouldn't I have done the same thing if I were his age?"

Farrun didn't answer with his usual soft growl or wet lick.

"I really messed up this time, didn't I? How are we going to free him?" Farrun still had no answer. "You can't follow them, but I have to. I want you to leave. Swing wide and head northwest. The desert soon turns into half-usable farmland. I'm sure you'll find something to eat, too. You remember when we used to play hide and seek? You always found me and ever since you've been a cub, you've never been too far away. They'll probably take Jeffrey to one of the villages near those fields; with luck, I'll be able to free him. Scout the villages and try to find us. If you can't, go to God's Hand Mountains. We'll meet you there. And this time, you be careful. If you're seen, there's no place to hide."

Farrun licked her face once and nuzzled her chin. Then he silently ran off, leaving Susan hugging her knees and feeling miserable.

In the morning, a Susan-rentia watched nine king's soldiers break camp. Though Jeffrey was untied to eat and drink, a soldier stood behind him the whole time with a knife to his neck. She heard the soldier behind Jeffrey complaining. "Why do I have to do this? The kid was half dead from the storm when he stumbled into our camp, and he can't be more than ten or eleven. What's he going to do, tell his mother on us? It's kind of silly holding a knife to him, isn't it?"

"I told you last night, orders from Ometerer and that's the same as orders from the king. This is the way all green-eyes are to be treated when their hands aren't tied behind their backs or spread apart like he was last night. They don't get burned until a shaman with written orders from Ometerer is done speaking to them. I don't understand it, either, but we're going to follow those orders."

"How long do we have to keep the boy?"

"Until a shaman with orders from Ometerer speaks to him."

"But I heard that most of our army is moving," said another man. "We might not find any shamans. Rumor has it A'aster wants to attack the Thoral Mountains."

"If that's true," said the man nearest to the Susan-rentia, startling the bird and making it fly from one unsaddled horse to another, "it makes no sense. In a few months, most of the passes in the Thorals will be snowed

149

in. I don't want to winter in those mountains."

For the briefest of seconds, hearing that an army was marching on her home broke Susan's concentration, and the Susan-rentia began to change back into human form. But the Susan-mind instantly fought back. The bird's wings stopped fluttering and the change reversed itself before anyone noticed the bird suddenly growing an inch then shrinking back to its regular size.

"You want to hear a rumor that's even crazier?" said another voice. "A'aster's new son, our future king, is supposed to have green eyes. If it's true, I wonder what Ometerer is going to do about that?"

"If you ask me, nothing's made sense since Ometerer became head shaman. Why, in the last month, over three hundred farmers have been drafted into our division. If A'aster wanted to attack a cornfield, then those farmers will do a lot of good. But what are they going to do the first time a man stands up to them with a sword? They'll turn and run, that's what."

"Well, the next time the king asks your advice, you tell him that," said one who was obviously the leader. "Now hurry up!"

By now, Jeffrey had finished. A soldier had tied him tightly to a saddle and squeezed onto the horse behind him. The soldiers began; the Susan-rentia followed. After half an hour, the land became more green than brown — they were entering the farm fields Susan had seen when she left the Elders' cave. She saw a village. *Fly to it. There will be water.* The Susan-rentia answered by turning slightly toward the houses.

If there are no shamans there, I'll be able to free Jeffrey.

The Susan-rentia circled the village. *Oh no — three . . . Vincent!* The bird fell from the sky almost to the ground and luckily, no one noticed. Her wings flapped and the Susan-rentia's dive turned into a quick landing on the windowsill of a small hut at the edge of the village. When she saw the hut was empty, she wanted to enter.

NO-NO-IN-SIDE.

Yes! and the Susan-rentia flew in. Once there, Susan became herself. Her mouth was dry, and in a quick look around, she saw that there was nothing to eat or drink in the hut. Staying by the window, she soon heard the clopping of horses' hooves. The soldiers dismounted; Jeffrey remained tied to the saddle.

"It's him!" Susan heard. "It's the witch-boy who escaped from Lief. I told you, Turop, he was hiding in God's Hand. I told you!"

"Yes, Vincent," said another voice, "you told us."

"Where's the other one?" demanded Vincent, pointing at Jeffrey.

The leader of the soldiers bowed his head slightly to the shaman. "What other one, Master? This is the only one we found."

"I wasn't talking to you," shouted Vincent. "I was talking to the witch-boy. I want to know where that witch-girl is!"

"I'm sorry, Master," said the leader, lifting his arms to stop Vincent from passing. "Before you speak to the boy, I have to see orders from Ometerer."

"Orders! You will turn him over to me at once! I want to know where the other one is."

"I'm sorry. I can't."

"Not to him," said Turop, "but to me. This is what you want, isn't it?"

The leader took a paper from the shaman. "That's the King's seal, Shaman Turop," he said, handing it back.

"See, Vincent, I told you not to get so excited. After we talk to the boy, you can have him. Then you can do whatever you want with him."

"Don't you understand, Turop? The witch-girl is near here. She killed Kenar. I know, I found the body. Ometerer said I could find the girl and the boy knows where she is. I want him now!"

"Vincent," said Turop, "do I have to remind you what else Ometerer said to you? I think our master understated your problem. The death of one possible witch-girl is not important. The work we do, the knowledge we seek, and the eventual destruction of all the green-eyes is. You will speak to the boy when we finish with him. Now get out of our way or I promise I will petition Ometerer to remove you from our order!"

Susan didn't know what to do. Even if she changed shape, there was no animal she knew of that could scatter so many armed soldiers. Suddenly she saw Vincent violently push Turop. "I am not a novice to be talked to this way. I will see the witch-boy now!" Turop cried out as he fell and several soldiers quickly ran to help pick him up.

The soldiers were soon busy. Vincent swung his bony arm in an attempt to hit the third shaman before Turop could get to his feet. That shaman struck back. Some of the soldiers were trying to separate the two shouting men, while others helped Turop stand and dusted off his white robe.

If I don't try to free Jeffrey now, I may never get another chance. Taking a deep breath and holding up the bottom of her dress, she ran out of the hut. She was able to get near the horses before anyone saw her, and the first shout went unnoticed because the soldiers were still trying to keep the shamans from fighting. By the time she was seen, Susan was scrambling up into the saddle of the horse next to Jeffrey. She grabbed the reins of his horse, kicked the one she was on, and screamed as loudly as she could.

The other horses scattered, the soldiers ran after them, and Susan heard one voice shouting over everything. "It's her! It's her!"

As soon as Susan and Jeffrey had cleared the village, she turned the horses to head back toward the desert. They had one chance — reach God's Hand before the soldiers caught them.

She looked at Jeffrey, who sort of smiled. His hands were securely tied to the pummel of the saddle, and even if Susan had had a knife, she couldn't stop to cut him free. So she urged her horse on, and Jeffrey helped by kicking his. When she turned back, she saw soldiers and two shamans following.

The horses ran, their feet pounding on the dry earth. Susan bounced in the saddle, not caring if she came down hard. "Let's go!" she yelled, "faster, faster!" The horses answered with a small burst of speed, but soon they tired and began to slow. Susan felt it and kicked out again. "You can't stop running now! Please, you can't." But the horses did and a gallop became a fast trot. Then she heard it; flying in the air after them, the faint sounds of chanting.

She looked back. The soldiers and shamans were still

153

about the same distance behind. "Jeffrey," she called. "Shout, holler, anything. Maybe if we can't hear the shamans, their magic won't hurt us."

"Yaaaaa! Yaaaaa!"

"That's it," shouted Susan, not knowing if he could hear her. "Faster, faster, faster!"

And so they all headed into the desert. The soldiers and chanting shamans, the screaming child and teenager, and horses that were slowly running themselves into exhaustion.

"Th–there! G–God's Hand. We're almost there."

Susan stopped shouting and looked up. They had just passed the beginning of the rocks. Wildly, she looked around for something to cut Jeffrey's ropes. But there was nothing. "Is the cave large enough for the horse?"

"I–I don't know! There! To the left. I stacked those r-rocks like that s–so we co–could find it."

As Susan turned her horse, it stumbled. It didn't fall, but its body twisted and threw her. Jeffrey and her horse continued on as the pursuing horses, mouths foaming white, charged.

Susan forgot to shout, and the hoarse chanting of the two shamans reached her. *At least Vincent isn't one of them,* she thought as her body froze.

Just then, she heard a familiar sound from behind the rocks guarding the secret entrance. Accompanied by a loud howl, a dark mass of fur flew up and across her vision. Landing in front of the horses, Farrun howled a second time and attacked. The horses veered and the shamans stopped chanting as they grabbed their saddle horns to keep from falling. Susan was instantly released and ran after Jeffrey, whose horse had stopped at the rock wall.

"Where's the key?" she shouted. "The sign!"

Jeffrey's throat was raw and Susan could barely hear him. "L–le–left . . . l–l–left, up . . . up, r–ri–right."

"Jeffrey!"

"There! Your r–right hand! Your r–right hand!"

Susan saw it, the horizontal eight. "Farrun!" Before pushing the sign to open the door, she ran for Jeffrey. "Farrun!" She looked up. The soldiers were off their horses — three of them racing toward her. The others, bows drawn, were shooting at Farrun, who was chasing the men coming toward Susan. "Farrun," Susan called again, "come on!" He turned sharply to avoid being hit by a second flight of arrows and raced to her. Susan pushed the rock where the lines of the Elders' mark came together. The rock door slid open; arrows aimed at her flew past her head. "Duck!" she shouted to Jeffrey. She led the horse in — Farrun ran by — the door slammed shut. Dark silence.

No one said anything. Susan leaned against the horse, feeling Farrun at her feet, hearing Jeffrey breathing as loudly as she was. The horse panted, too, too tired, too exhausted to smell the wolf next to it. Eventually the light came on, and still no one moved or said anything. Finally, Susan, her dress soaked with sweat, looked up at Jeffrey and spoke in slow, even tones. "Jeff . . . Jeffrey, if you ever leave again before you are fully trained, I will spank you so hard you won't sit down for a month."

Farrun growled loud enough for him to hear.

Jeffrey didn't answer. Susan saw his face was drained of all color. He slowly nodded his head, and she had enough energy to nod hers back.

When she had recovered a little, she unbuckled the saddle and helped steady Jeffrey as she pulled it off. In the saddlebag she found a cloth, and slowly began wiping the horse down as Farrun gnawed at the rope securing Jeffrey. If he nipped Jeffrey, Susan never knew it. The boy didn't make a sound.

When she finished with the horse, Jeffrey was sitting away from Farrun, leaning against the wall. Susan plopped down next to him. He didn't move until she put her arm around him; then he turned into her chest and cried. Susan hugged him as tightly as she could. She kissed his head and stroked his wet hair. "It's all right, now, brother, you're safe. You're back with me. It's all right. We're all together." Farrun came and put his head down, half on her lap, half on his. Jeffrey put his arms around her, hugged her back, and continued to cry.

It was a long, slow walk back to the tub room, and when they reached it, Susan pulled off her dress and plunged in. Jeffrey joined her, with his clothes on, while the horse and Farrun each took a long, long drink.

Chapter 14

Later, while they ate the few journey cakes Susan had found in the saddlebag, she asked Jeffrey one question. "Why did you do it?"

"I–I th–th–th–"

"It's all right, Jeffrey," she interrupted. "I'm not angry anymore. Relax and take your time. Besides, I don't think you'll do it again."

"I didn't want you to go alone. It was too da–dangerous. I wanted to show you I wasn't a baby and could help. I'm sorry — I should have listened to you."

Susan stared at Jeffrey, who was sitting against the opposite wall. He was still half wet, naked, except for a cloth over his middle, and looked more like ten than the twelve he was.

"I'm sorry, too," she said. "I should have listened to you." When Jeffrey looked puzzled, she explained. "You taught me something when I saved Maria. You told me that sometimes rules have to change. I thought you were right then, but I didn't have the courage to do it when I should have. I told you once that I thought you have more power than I do. I should have tried to teach you to become a rentia. I should have been willing to take a chance. Because I didn't, you became your panther and left. I think we were both wrong, but luckily, it worked out all right. From now on, we do things together. That way, I hope, neither of us will make any big mistakes."

Farrun looked up from the corner he was napping in, growled softly, and put his head back down.

"If I make a decision that you don't like, you tell me. We'll talk it over and decide what to do together. If it means bending a rule in order to do what we have to, then we bend the rule. All right, Clan-brother?"

"All right, Clan-sister. And speaking of Maria, when this is all over, can we go to Kestra? Maria said that she'd ask Befany to teach us. Knowing how to heal with magic is a good idea."

"You're right," answered Susan. "If this Befany will teach us, maybe we can learn more than just healing. Maybe we can learn how to fight the shamans' magic. Several times Maria asked me if I used dark magic. That must be the kind of magic the shamans use. But dark magic has to have an opposite — a light magic, a good magic. If we can learn that, then we have a better chance of defeating the shamans and protecting our clan. But we have more important things to do first. When this is all over, and Ometerer is dead, then we'll talk about going to Kestra.

"Here," she said, standing and throwing Jeffrey a pair of pants and a shirt from the saddlebag, "until your clothes dry, wear these. They'll be really big on you, but they'll have to do."

He went out in the corridor to change while Susan sad-

158

dled the horse. "Why can't we wait for my clothes to dry?" he asked when he came back.

Susan tried hard not to laugh, but she wasn't very successful. "We have to find grazing for the horse, Farrun must be hungry and has to hunt for his dinner, and I want to get back to the Thorals."

"Then we aren't going to Nieswim's castle?"

Susan shook her head. "You remember what the soldiers who captured you said? The king's army is moving toward the Thorals. If that's true, I think Ometerer will be with them."

"Why?"

"I heard Ometerer talk to Vincent. The head shaman suspects our power, but he's also smart enough to know that not everyone with green eyes has it. If Ometerer wants to learn for himself what we can do, then I think he'll go where most of us live — the Thoral Mountains."

"That makes sense. And I just remembered what Lord Falcon said about Ometerer never staying in one place for a long time. Even if we don't find him with the army, he has probably left Nieswim's castle."

They had to move quickly because the door stayed open only a short time. Lining up in front of it, Jeffrey pushed the Elders' sign and the door slid open. Farrun jumped straight to the valley floor just in case anything threatening was there. Jeffrey was next, dragging the horse after him. As soon as the horse was on the ledge, the boy jumped, pulling it with him. The only one to lag was Susan. She saw the horse leap and stepped out. But instead of following right away, she paused, looking at the dead land. *Nothing's changed.*

"Look out!" called Jeffrey.

Susan looked back just as the door closed, clamping shut on the bottom of her dress.

"I told you to watch out," said a laughing Jeffrey.

Susan kneeled down and pulled at the material, trying to get it out. *Come on!* But the dress didn't listen. "Will you open up!" The wall didn't listen either. She yanked harder. Most of her dress came free, but a small, half-moon piece of it remained stuck in the wall.

She looked down at Farrun, who was making small, whining noises. They weren't growls, but they weren't yelps, either.

"Go ahead," she said to the wolf. "Laugh at me, too. But who do you think is going to have to steal me a new dress?" Before finally jumping off the ledge, Susan picked at the cloth until nothing could be seen. While she was doing that, Jeffrey piled rocks neatly under the ledge to mark the door.

They rode the horse toward Lief and camped next to the stream Susan and Jeffrey had walked in when they were running from Vincent. After the fire was started and they were sitting next to it, Susan put her arm over Farrun's shoulder, scratched his ear, and said to him in a soft voice, "Farrun, how about sneaking into Lief and getting me something to wear?"

Farrun stood. He walked to the stream and took a long drink without looking up.

"I don't think he's going to go," said Jeffrey. "But my clothes are dry."

"They're a little small for me, don't you think?"

160

"But these aren't." Jeffrey pointed to the soldier's clothes he had on.

"I can't shape-change in them. They've been dyed that brown color. I'd have to take them off before I changed, and I'd be naked when I became me again."

Farrun trotted over to her and pushed her toward Jeffrey. "I know what you want," she said. "If I become my she-wolf, I'll have to stay that way until I find a place to change back that happens to have some clothes nearby."

Farrun grabbed her dress in his mouth and shook his head. Susan pulled it away, forgetting about Farrun's sharp teeth. The wolf sat in front of her with a large part of the bottom of the dress in his mouth. He looked very pleased with himself as he shook his head, growled, and let the cloth flap against his face. The growl wasn't very loud because the cloth muffled the sound. Susan changed into the soldier's clothes.

Farrun disappeared just long enough to catch their dinner, and that was only a small rabbit. The one thing that the soldier didn't have in his bag was a knife, so the rabbit was roasted whole, fur and all. It wasn't the best meal they had ever eaten, but it filled their stomachs. Sometime during the night Farrun poked Susan and ran off. He was hungry and wanted her to stay awake while he found his own dinner. She put some more wood on the fire and waited for him to return.

In the morning, she spoke to Jeffrey. "The Thoral Mountains are in southern Reune. The safest way to get to them is from the west because the land isn't so good and

161

not too many people live there. The farther east you go, the more people you find."

"Where are we?" he asked.

Susan drew a map of Reune on the ground. It looked sort of like a large oval with flattened ends. "This is the Endless Sea," she said, pointing to the western border. "The Thundrous Mountains are here, taking up a good part of our eastern border. And here, on the bottom, halfway between the sea and the eastern border, are the Thoral Mountains."

"Where are *we*?" Jeffrey repeated.

"We're here, near God's Hand," she said, putting her finger down near the center of the oval.

"B–but that means . . ."

"The Thorals are due south, right through some of the best farmland in all of Reune."

"B–but how are we going . . ."

Susan scratched her head. Then she drew a line from where her finger was straight down to the Thoral Mountains.

Farrun, who was sitting next to them, growled. When Susan looked at him he snapped at the air between their faces.

"He doesn't like it," Jeffrey said.

"We don't have a choice. If we go west first, it will take us an extra three or four weeks. If the army is moving, we have to get home as soon as we can. What do you think?"

Jeffrey looked at the dirt map. "I think she's right, Farrun," he said to the wolf.

Farrun bit the air again, making a loud clicking noise with his teeth.

"He still doesn't like it," said Jeffrey, petting him.

"Neither do I," she answered.

They began after a breakfast of water from the stream. Farrun led, trying to keep them away from any villages. He managed to do that for the first couple of days because the ground was rocky and not too many people farmed it. When they did pass a field, Susan and Jeffrey were able to steal enough to keep their stomachs from talking back. But after the third day, they were forced to stop. The ground dropped, sloping steeply for one or two hundred feet. From where Susan stood, it looked as if some fantastically large giant had scooped up the top layer of land stretching into the horizon. All she could see were green fields, houses, and smoke from fires.

"What now?" asked Jeffrey.

Farrun answered. He walked back and lay down next to the largest rock in the half-open field they had just crossed.

"From now on, we travel at night," she said, going to Farrun. "I don't think I could convince him otherwise." She tied the horse to a bush so it could graze and went to sit next to Jeffrey and Farrun.

They must have dozed off because they suddenly woke to the sound of horses. Farrun growled as he faced the sound. His back hair was up, and his teeth were showing.

"We can't outrun the horses," she said quietly, as she saw a troop of soldiers coming toward them. Her heart raced, her voiced quickened. "We can't shape-change, either. The soldiers would see us and there's nothing for us to hide behind while we do it. Get out of here, Farrun, hide in the fields below. Quickly, they've got bows. Hide, Farrun, hide!" She pushed Farrun, and looking back once, the wolf ran for the slope. Susan put her arm tightly around Jeffrey and waited for the soldiers.

"Two of them this time, Captain," said one of the soldiers to his officer. The one with the captain's helmet shook his head when he saw them.

"Children! The king wants us to war on children." Susan saw him spit on the ground. "Was that your dog we saw running away?" Susan nodded her head. "Be thankful he ran. We would have had to kill him if he had stayed. Where are you from?"

Susan swallowed. "The Thoral Mountains."

"Where were you born?" he asked.

"Lief," answered Jeffrey.

"You've come a long way without being caught. Now listen, I've got orders about how to treat captive green-eyes, but you're just kids and I don't want to tie you up that tightly. You're not going to do anything foolish, are you?" Susan slowly shook her head. "Good. You," he said, pointing to Susan, "ride with me. Treenaw, you take the boy."

Several of the soldiers dismounted, and Susan soon found herself sitting uncomfortably in front of the captain with her hands bound loosely behind her back. The captain led his company of men slowly down the slope and between the rows of almost ripe crops.

What am I going to do? They'll kill me if I don't escape. But I can't shape-change now. Then they'll know for sure what we can do. And what about Jeffrey? The only thing he can become is a panther, and if he did, there'd be no place for him to hide. Why didn't I teach him to become a bird? I can't leave him. I just can't!

When they reached the village, the captain dismounted and helped Susan down. "There are no shamans here," he said, "and we have to keep you until one of them with orders shows up. Then . . ." He led them to a small house on the side of the village. Inside, Susan saw two poles sunk deep into the ground. "I'm . . . sorry about this," said the captain as Susan's ropes were undone. "Your hands and feet are going to be tied to those poles. Someone will come in to let you walk around and feed you. But the rest of the time you're going to be strapped. It's going to be hard enough explaining why you aren't tied tighter with your arms and legs spread out as far as they can go without breaking. There will be guards outside at all times. If you get thirsty, just call."

"How long are we going to be here?" asked Susan as she was tied to the poles, back to back with Jeffrey.

The captain shook his head. "I haven't seen the shaman in ten days. He's overdue." He opened his mouth to continue, but must have decided against it. He waited until his men finished and then left.

Once they were alone, Jeffrey whispered to her. "Change. You g–get away."

"How would you explain my escape? Don't you think the shaman would know I used the power?"

"B–but at least you'll be safe."

"I won't leave you, Jeffrey."

"B–but . . ."

165

"Listen to me, Clan-brother. We are staying together. I could change with my hands and feet tied like this, but you can't. You can only become your panther. If I freed you from the ropes, you'd be seen leaving the hut. That would be just as bad as the shaman finding you alone."

"But Ometerer knows anyway. You said that yourself."

"He may know, but most of the people in Reune don't. Seeing a panther leave here would let everyone in this village know about the power. No, Jeffrey, if we have to change, we do it when we have no other choice. Agreed?"

"But you should . . ."

"Jeffrey!"

"All right." In the silence that followed, Susan was sure she heard her heart beating loudly. Several times, she felt Jeffrey lean his head back and push against her. Once, he sort of cried but turned it into a cough instead.

"It's all right to be afraid, Jeffrey. I'm scared, too."

Several hours later, five soldiers came in. They untied the captives, stood guard while they ate and drank, and re-tied them before leaving. Just before sunset, the soldiers came back and repeated the procedure. The only difference was that when they left Susan and Jeffrey were lying down, tied to posts hammered into the ground.

Morning came early, and when it did, Susan was sorry. Something kicked her side and when her eyes didn't open immediately, the kick came again. *White . . . a white robe!*

"Why are the ropes so loose?" the shaman asked. "Why aren't their arms and legs spread further apart?"

"They're only children," answered the captain.

"Do you set yourself above the law, Captain?"

"No, Shaman Horinjer. It will not happen again."

166

"Bring them," said Horinjer. The shaman turned on his heels and left.

Jeffrey and Susan were taken to the largest house in the village; unlike the one-room huts, this house had three rooms. Horinjer was waiting, sitting in a wooden chair, slowly sipping something from a steaming cup. He put the cup on the floor and told the soldiers to leave.

Susan watched him stare at her and Jeffrey. Her hands were tied tightly behind her back and a length of short cord was attached from her wrists to her ankles, making it impossible for her to stand straight.

"Being tied like that is not very comfortable," said the shaman. "But my questioning will be quick. Afterward, the soldiers can get on with their jobs."

"What do you want?" asked Susan.

"I hope you know. If you do, you will live. If you don't, you'll soon be dead and it won't matter."

"I don't understand."

Horinjer reached down and took a crossbow from behind the chair. Suddenly its string was pulled back and an arrow was lying in the notch. "I have never understood why I need this," he said, "but Ometerer, in his wisdom, would never have ordered it unless it was necessary. Now, listen to the words of Ometerer, Head of the Shamans, Defender of the True Magic." Susan saw him close his eyes as he thought. "There is among the people, whose ancestors started an unsuccessful bid to rule Reune, a certain power. All those with their ancestors' sign, those whose eyes are green, are to be told this. Show your power to the shaman before you, and you shall be brought to me. Do nothing and you will be burned at the stake."

167

"What are you asking?" whispered Susan.

The shaman leaned back in his chair and looked out the window. "The wood will have been stacked by now. If you can show me something that will make me believe you have a power beyond what normal people can do, you will live. If not, you will die." Now Horinjer stood up and lowered the crossbow. "They never do, you know, show me a power. Ometerer is very secretive about what the power is. Only a handful of his closest advisers are supposed to know. But still, I will sell the horse that was captured with you. That will pay for my time. Since it wasn't a very good horse, I will not spend much time with you."

He walked back to the window. "Just as I thought. Everything is ready."

"I can't show you tied like this," said Susan.

"Su–su–"

"Quiet, boy! Can't show me what?"

"The power."

Horinjer stared at her. "You mean it, don't you? Yes, I see it in your eyes. You know what this means, if you are telling the truth. I'll be the first. Ometerer will make me one of his advisers. I'll be able to stop riding from dirt village to dirt village and live in a real city. But if you're lying to me, you'll die very slowly."

"I can't do it with my hands tied and I can't do it in these clothes."

"What do clothes have to do with it!"

Susan turned around so the shaman could cut her hands free. When she turned back again, Horinjer was pointing the crossbow at her head. "What will happen to my brother?"

"Whatever happens to you. Well, get on with it. Show me this power Ometerer wants so badly he's willing to kill half the people in the Thoral Mountains to get."

"I told you, I can't do anything in these clothes. I'd like a dress."

"You were serious about that?"

Susan nodded.

While Horinjer called the soldiers and told them what to get, Jeffrey whispered to Susan.

"Why show him? Become a rentia and fly away. Save yourself."

"No," said Susan, "not if it means your death. You heard what he said. No one knows about the power. He won't tell anyone until we reach Ometerer. Maybe we'll think of something before we reach him. All right?"

Jeffrey nodded.

I'm sorry, Rillan.

The soldiers brought three dresses. Two were almost her size and one was much too big. All were undyed wool.

"Change," Horinjer said, after the soldiers left.

Susan looked up at him.

"You have enough to worry about without concerning yourself with a man watching you undress."

Susan turned her back to him and pulled off her shirt. Then she slipped one of the dresses over her head and took off her pants.

"Now," said the shaman, holding the crossbow up and pointing it at her. "Show me the power."

Susan looked at Jeffrey, who half smiled at her. Then she closed her eyes. When she opened them, the shaman was staring at a full-grown she-wolf.

Chapter 15

"Enough!" shouted Horinjer. "Enough or I'll kill the boy!" The Susan-wolf vanished and Susan stood in its place. "Impossible," said the shaman, sitting down and shaking his head. The crossbow shook in his hand. "Can the boy . . ."

"No," answered Susan. "The power is very rare."

"Ometerer will decide, and I will be there with him. I will be there! You are to tell no one of this, do you understand? Guards!"

When the guards came in, he shouted orders to them. "The two prisoners and I are leaving immediately for Ometerer's camp. Tell the captain to assemble his entire company. You will ride with us. These two will be chained to a wagon and watched at all times. Do you understand?"

"Yes, Master," answered the two men who stood before him.

"The chains are tight," whispered Horinjer into Susan's ear before they left. "The wolf's paw would be crushed. Do you understand?" Susan nodded.

For the next twelve days, Susan and Jeffrey remained chained to the wagon and in all that time, they were unable to come up with a plan so they could both escape. The one thing that kept Susan from being completely depressed was that every night, when the twin moons were high in the sky, a lone wolf could be heard howling nearby.

On the eighth day, Susan saw the shadow in the distance that marked the beginning of the Thoral Mountains. On the ninth day, the tallest peaks, poking white, snow-covered heads above the clouds, stood before her. On the tenth day, the green hills and tall pine trees were visible.

On the last day before reaching Grogen Pass, something strange happened. Susan was jolted awake just after dawn. Though there were only light puffy clouds above, a single thunderclap crashed over the camp. Everyone was up instantly. Susan and Jeffrey looked at the sky along with the soldiers and shaman, but no one saw anything except birds frightened into sudden flight.

When they stopped for lunch, Jeffrey asked, "What's Grogen Pass?"

"The Thorals are very wide," Susan answered, "and there are hundreds of places where roads or paths lead up into the mountains. Most of them start in the foothills and wind their way up. If you wanted to enter the mountains with an army, horses would have a hard time getting up some of the steeper paths, and the soldiers would have to walk in single file. They would be easy to defeat. But Grogen Pass is different. It's a huge plain. If you stay in the center of it, you are far enough away from the sides so no one can throw rocks down at you. The plain narrows slightly at the end and then widens like a fan. There are eight roads at the end of the fan, each one leading into the mountains. No one knows who made those roads, maybe the Elders did, maybe people who were here even before the Elders. If A'aster's army takes control of Grogen Pass, he can send his soldiers to many of the villages and keep them supplied while they fight."

"Ometerer must be there," said Jeffrey. "At least we were right when we guessed he would be with the army."

Susan wanted to hug him but they were chained to opposite sides of the wagon. "I'm sure the people of the Thorals are there, too. Maklin told me the main reason our ancestors weren't completely destroyed was that enough of them survived to hold the advancing king's army in the pass. When winter set in, the king's army left. That's when one of the generals went to the king and signed a treaty."

"Do you think the people of the Thorals can hold off A'aster's army?"

"There's a big difference between people and an army." They finished the rest of their lunch in silence.

Reaching A'aster's camp at the entrance to Grogen Pass, the mountains loomed in front of them. Susan felt glad when she saw the huge trees that grew on the lower slopes. But then her breath deepened; her eyes shut.

This is not the way I dreamed of coming home from my testing period; in chains, without Farrun, and giving away the secret that has been guarded since before the time of the rebellion: proof of the power. Jeffrey asked why her eyes were red, but Susan didn't answer.

The king's army was large. From her wagon, Susan saw hundreds of campfires, horses, men, wagons flooded with full sacks and closed barrels. The farmers who worked the land near Grogen Pass would go hungry this winter because their fields had been completely overrun by the invading army. Immediately after they arrived, Horinjer disappeared. Even before the blacksmiths removed the chains holding Susan and Jeffrey to the wagon, the shaman reappeared with three other men in white. Two soldiers with crossbows were also with them.

"If you turn, or walk in any direction other than where we walk, the boy will be shot," said Horinjer to Susan. But before they started, the three shamans moved closer and stared at her.

"We finally have one," whispered a small shaman. "The master spoke the truth! Now our power will be complete. Praise Ometerer, Defender of the True Magic."

They didn't know for sure! They didn't know. If I am the first, it's possible Ometerer just guessed! But now all the shamans will know. Even if I kill Ometerer and destroy the scroll, they will know and continue Ometerer's war without him. What have I done?

Susan and Jeffrey were ushered into a large tent set up at the edge of the army. They were led behind a cloth partition and told to wait.

"But your Majesty," said a voice loudly from the other side of the divider, "it is madness to attack the Thorals this late in the summer. Even if they don't defend the pass, it will take us a month to establish bases in the low-lying villages, and one more to move all the supplies to them. Our men will be trapped by the first heavy snow. At least a third of my army are untrained farmers. How do you expect them to fight in the snow?"

173

Susan heard a soft, almost feminine voice, answer in a straight monotone. "We . . . have . . . de . . . ci . . . ded. You . . . will . . . do . . . as . . . we . . . wish."

"Did you hear, General?" said another voice. Susan recognized it — Ometerer.

"Then at least give me a reason to tell my men why they fight."

"Because," answered Ometerer, "your king wishes it."

"But your Majesty!" objected the general.

"I . . . wish . . . it."

"Yes, Majesty," said the general. He bumped into one of the shamans near Susan as he backed out. When he turned and saw whom he had touched, Susan noticed the look of hate in the general's face. The shamans rushed forward, and the soldier behind Susan poked her in the back with an arrow tip to get her moving.

The first figure she saw was A'aster. He didn't look very kingly, slumped in his throne, dressed in a blue and gold shirt that was much too big. A pale face with hollow cheeks and glazed eyes looked at Susan.

"Which is the one?" she heard, and turned to the voice. In contrast to the king, Ometerer was tall, almost six feet, stocky, with full-rounded cheeks, a clean-shaven face and head, and a spotless white robe.

"The girl, Master," said Horinjer.

"You will now see, your Majesty, why this war is necessary. You will see with your own eyes the power of the witches that has caused droughts on your land and the unexplained illness that has robbed you of your health. You will see, too, why I must take your son. The witches must be destroyed."

"My . . . son."

"We will discuss that matter later, your Majesty.

"My . . . son."

Susan saw Ometerer step closer to the king and whisper something in his ear.

"Yes . . . O . . . me . . . ter . . . er. We . . . will . . . talk . . . la . . . ter.

I AM the first! Of all the people they've killed, no one has shown them the power. And Ometerer IS controlling the king. He must have the king under a spell. Think, Susan! Maklin taught me to use my head. Now use it! Think . . . think!

Jeffrey leaned into her and when she looked down, he smiled.

"Show us your power, witch, and you shall not die."

"Don't," whispered Jeffrey very quietly.

Susan took a breath. The arrow pressed into her back. She took a step forward, closed her eyes, and then relaxed. When she opened them, Susan was still Susan. "No," she said to Ometerer. "Not while my brother is a captive."

"You will do as I say or the boy dies," answered Ometerer.

"No," said the king. "I . . . will . . . see. Free . . . the . . . boy."

Ometerer took one step toward her. Then he looked at Horinjer.

"I swear, Master Ometerer, I saw what I saw."

Ometerer nodded slowly and the soldier behind Jeffrey grabbed him. "No," said Susan. "I don't trust you. I want to see Jeffrey given a horse and ride into the pass. Then I'll do as you ask."

175

Again, Ometerer stepped closer to Susan. He reached into his robe and pulled out a long scroll case. He opened the case and carefully began removing the scroll.

He's going to put a spell on me! "I can't be forced into this. Whatever you read from that scroll will do no good." Susan didn't know if she believed it or not, but she stood tall and stared into Ometerer's eyes.

He pushed the scroll back into the case. "Do as she wishes. But keep both bows on her back."

"I'm not leaving . . ."

"Yes, you are," said Susan, turning and pulling him close. "Listen to me, Jeffrey, you are going to get on a horse and get out of here. You are going to save yourself. Do you understand?"

Susan held his hand tightly as they waited for someone to bring Jeffrey a horse. When it came, Susan bent down and hugged him.

"I love you," he whispered to her.

"And I you, little Clan-brother. That's why you're leaving."

"I'm coming back for you," he whispered. "If Ometerer hurts you, I'll kill him."

Susan moved away and looked into his eyes. She was about to tell him not to do it when she realized it wouldn't do any good. Though Jeffrey hadn't been taught to use his power fully, these last few months had not been easy for him; it was almost as if he was on his testing period, too. He didn't need someone to say "no" to him. He needed someone to guide him, to watch him. "Find Farrun," she said as she hugged him one last time. "He's somewhere. Talk to him. You'll have to figure out his answers, but he'll know what to do. He always knows." She wiped her eyes as he got on a horse and rode all alone into the opening of Grogen Pass. When she felt an arrow stabbing her, she walked back to the king's tent.

Ometerer met her at the entrance. "The king is sleeping and will rest for several hours. You will perform for me in my tent, and when the king is ready, you will show him."

"No," said Susan again. "I promised you I would show you my power, and I will keep my word. But I'll do it only once. After that, you can burn me or cut me into pieces or torture me any way you want. I will show you one time, and you, the king, and the four shamans shall watch."

"You are a brave little witch," he said, "but a foolish one. I will let you have your moment of triumph, for now.

"Tie her tightly, arms and legs spread far apart," he said to the soldiers. "You see," Ometerer said, turning to the four shamans, "I have always said that if one magic exists on Enstor, then why not two or three. We know the scroll-spells are real. And soon, we will know for sure that the ancient stories about the green-eyes are also true."

Susan had time to think, several hours' worth. Though she could escape by becoming a snake or another small animal that could slip through the ropes cutting into her arms and legs, she decided not to. Escaping didn't matter. Killing Ometerer and destroying the scroll did. To do that, she had to get rid of the soldiers that always followed him. She didn't want them to see the performance she had planned. When they came for her, the sun had set, and the twin moons were only beginning to light the sky. Torches lit the king's tent when Susan was brought there.

"Well, witch, show the king your power."

"Tell the soldiers to leave," she said.

"Now that is stupid," answered Ometerer. "They will watch with their bows aimed at you."

"Then they will watch nothing!" said Susan.

"Clear . . . the . . . tent. Eve . . . ry . . . bod . . . y . . . out. Now," said the king.

Before Ometerer could open his mouth, the soldier behind Susan turned and shouted, "Clear the tent. By order of the King, clear the tent!"

Ometerer reached behind him and picked up a crossbow. "Go ahead, witch. Show the king."

Ometerer was probably expecting a wolf and aimed his arrow low, to the height of a wolf's chest. But Susan had already decided against that. The plan she had thought of was simple. She would become an insect, a common fly. She had practiced that a long time ago and knew that insects were easy to control. The men watching would never notice her land next to Ometerer before turning into a snake. Earlier, a snake's instincts had slayed a man. But this time, no matter how distasteful it was for Susan, the calculated plan of a Shape-Changer would kill. Ometerer had to die and Susan knew it. The scroll would be next. When he fell, she would crawl into his robe and bite through the case. The snake's poison would dissolve the scroll. She didn't plan after that.

"Well," said Ometerer, "show the king your power."

Susan closed her eyes, and just as she began to concentrate, it happened. She was knocked aside when two shapes jumped into the room. One half-grown panther, sleek and shiny black, silently leaped past her. He landed high on Ometerer's chest and raked his rear claws down.

As blood soaked into the robe, the Jeffrey-panther grabbed Ometerer by his throat and shut off his death cry. Even as they fell, the Jeffrey-panther's front and back claws continued to push and rip at Ometerer's chest, tearing the scroll case and letting blood cover the paper.

Susan turned to the four shamans, staring wide-eyed as their leader died, too frightened to move. But Farrun wasn't frightened. As silently as the Jeffrey-panther, he grabbed the closest shaman, the one who had brought Susan, and bit the man's throat open. Before that man had time to fall, Farrun had sprung at another. Susan ran to the fallen crossbow and shot it, bringing down the third shaman. The Jeffrey-panther was about to charge the last one, when the general and several armed soldiers poured into the room.

"Stop!" shouted Susan. "They are my pets! They won't hurt the king. Listen to me! Listen to me!"

Farrun and the Jeffrey-panther stood before Susan. They faced the soldiers, one hissing, one growling, both showing white teeth still wet with blood.

"What are you waiting for!" shouted the last shaman, finding his voice. "She is a witch! She made them appear out of the air. Kill her!"

As the soldiers stepped forward, Susan ran to the general. "The witch *is* dead," she said, pointing at Ometerer. "He put the king under a spell. He wanted the power for himself. I heard what you said about this war and how you feel about it. You said yourself it makes no sense. Ometerer wanted the war. He used magic on A'aster to get his way. All the shamans want to do is get richer and they're destroying our country to do it." Susan ran to Ometerer's body and ripped what was left of the scroll case from the strap still around his shoulder. "Ometerer used this, a scroll of magic words to put a spell on our king."

"The scroll. Our magic!" croaked the shaman, seeing the destroyed paper.

"Listen . . . to . . . her," whispered the king.

That was all the general needed to hear. "Your magic did this?" he said to the shaman, pointing up and out, toward the mountains behind him, "Your magic!" Staring straight into the shaman's paling face, the general spoke softly to his men. "Round up all the shamans who march with the army. Gag them. Tightly. Strip them naked to make sure they have no weapons, bind their hands and feet, and leave them in the fields until morning. Send word to all my officers. Tomorrow, those companies not assigned to this area are to return home. All farmers drafted into the army are to be released. Tell them they may keep the horses we gave them. If they hurry, they might be able to return to their homes before the harvest.

"Next, send riders carrying flags of truce into the pass at first light. Tell the people in the hills that reason has returned to the throne and we wish to talk to . . ."

"By what right do you do this!" interrupted the shaman. "With Ometerer's death, I, Kilitor, am head of the shamans. My word, General, not yours, is second only to the king. How dare you presume to give orders!"

The general looked at the king, who was slowly shaking his head. Then the general turned and squarely faced the shaman. When he spoke, his voice was low, but each word was punched out to make sure Kilitor heard it. "By my commission as general of the army of Reune, and until

180

the king regains his health or the prince celebrates his eighteenth birthday, I rule in the king's name for the good of all the people. And, Shaman, I have ordered you gagged!"

The soldiers jumped the shaman, and before he could utter the first syllable of a spell, part of his own robe was stuffed into his mouth.

"Get these bodies out of here," said the general, walking to the king.

Susan returned to Farrun and the Jeffrey-panther. Both of them were still hissing and growling. She petted them at the same time, using long, hard strokes starting at their necks and ending by their tails. "Concentrate Jeffrey," she whispered, "stay your panther. Stay your panther. You did it. I'm so proud of you, Jeffrey. I'm proud of both of you." When Farrun and the Jeffrey-panther were calm enough to be left alone, Susan went to the king. He was still sitting in the same position, staring glassy-eyed at his general.

"Rest, your Majesty," said the general. "I will get my healer, the one Ometerer had refused to let see you these past three years. You'll get better now." The general rose, but seeing that none of his soldiers was there, kneeled back down.

"I'll watch him while you get the healer," said Susan.

The man looked at Farrun and the Jeffrey-panther standing next to Susan, silent, but with lips pulled back showing gleaming teeth.

"They only wanted to protect me. They won't harm the king."

"Go," whispered the king.

Ometerer's death broke the spell, and the shaman who

181

saw me use the power is dead. My clan is safe. All the green-eyes are safe. The king slumped in his chair and would have fallen if Susan hadn't caught him. She helped him sit on the floor by stretching his feet out. When he lifted his head, the glazed look from his eyes was gone.

"Thank . . . you, child," he whispered.

"Majesty," said the general, entering with four soldiers and a man in a beige robe.

"General Crypol," whispered the king. "I am glad . . . you're back."

"And I, Majesty," said the general, kneeling, "am glad you are back." They carried the king out, leaving Susan, the Jeffrey-panther, and Farrun, who had only now begun to lick her face.

Three days later, a weak king, with healthy eyes and a large appetite, sat in his tent. Next to him was General Crypol. In front of them sat Susan and Jeffrey, with Farrun sandwiched between, and eight men from the eight villages closest to Grogen Pass. The general read from a scroll, and each of the eight men read along on their own copies.

"The King of Reune, in recognition of the wrongs done to the people of the Thoral Mountains, and especially to those with green eyes, hereby grants the following:

"For the next twenty-five years, though each village must swear allegiance to the crown of Reune as they have always done, no taxes of any nature will be collected from any village in the Thoral Mountains.

"Second, the Order of the Shamans is outlawed. All shamans are to be arrested, brought to a camp that will be set up, and will remain there for the rest of their lives. Any shaman wishing to leave must agree to have his tongue cut out, so never again will he poison the people with evil magic.

"Third, all the wealth of the Order of the Shamans shall be distributed among the green-eyed citizens of Reune who lost their homes or relatives. Those citizens living outside the Thorals will be given eight months to state their losses to the crown and receive their compensation. At the conclusion of those eight months, the remaining wealth of the Order of the Shamans shall be delivered to Grogen Pass, and the people of the Thorals will distribute it among themselves.

"Thus it is agreed."

After the nine scrolls were signed, the king rose. "Thank you all," he said. As he was helped away, he stopped before Susan and Jeffrey. "I'm glad you found your brother."

"Thank you, your Majesty," answered Susan.

"Where is your other pet?" he asked, looking at Farrun. Susan looked up at the king. "Tell me," he asked, not waiting for her answer, "what is the power that Ometerer wanted me to see? What power do you hold over the animals that made them risk their lives for you?"

"Love, your Majesty," she answered quickly.

The king smiled. Farrun wagged his tail rapidly as he licked the faces of Susan and Jeffrey, one after the other.